The Search for Ethan

for Ethan

Robert Cowan

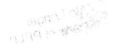

CHAPTER 1

Jean Slater's eyes opened slowly as she gradually re-entered the world, sighing gently as her early afternoon Mills and Boon daydream was replaced by her dimly lit council terrace living room and a faint hint of damp. She hated that smell. She'd always prided herself on keeping a clean house and this was like an itch she couldn't scratch. The council inspector had just shrugged his shoulders and promised to see what he could do. Six months later, that didn't appear to be very much. So, she learned to live with it, as just another thing she could do nothing about. She winced as she rose up in her black corduroy armchair, her long grey hair seeming to whiten with the effort. Only a year earlier it had been deep chestnut brown framing the face of a vibrant thirty nine year old woman, yet months of debilitating back pain had worn her down, draining her of life, carving pain into a face that had aged a generation.

"You ok, Ma?"

"Fine, son," she replied faintly. She had grown accustomed to lying. How many times could you complain without feeling a burden? She knew neither her son nor her husband felt that way, proven by deeds as well as words. Many times she'd thanked God for them, as many times as she'd had reason to curse Him for the life she now endured, but never had. A devout Catholic, she felt only guilt that she could no longer attend mass, feelings Father Ryan did his best to dispel on his regular visits.

"I'm away to school. See you at lunchtime."

"Okay son," she replied, pride momentarily dulling her pain. She watched through the window as her son ran to catch up with the dark haired boy swaggering slowly up ahead, feet weighed down by resentment. Her son Tommy and Stephen McDaid had been friends for as long as they could walk, but Jean had always had misgivings about her son's alliance. In her eyes Stephen was arrogant, rude, selfish, untrustworthy - everything Tommy wasn't - but she'd always felt there was more, something just under the surface, out of sight. Not good enough for her son, that was for sure, but what could she do? Slowly, she sat back in her chair, wincing with each sword thrust through her spine. Just as she began to nod off again, she was jolted back to consciousness by a loud knock and the door being opened sharply.

"It's just me, Jean."

Into the living room she strode, purple tracksuit, pink trainers, dyed blonde hair and vodka breath. There was nothing sober about Margo McDaid, even at 9 am.

"How are you today?"

"Fine, Margo, fine" Jean used to find her manic neighbour fun, full of life and with a heart of gold, but these days Jean just didn't have the energy. Some days she still brought a smile to her face, others she was overwhelming, or just plain crazy. She thought back to when Tommy was just beginning to talk.

"Mad!" he'd yell, pointing at Margo, having heard it whispered under his mother's breath once too often.

"You're right wee man," she'd reply, grabbing the child by the ankles, swinging him around and around, head barely missing the walls as they both laughed hysterically. It seemed a lifetime ago now, but Margo's verbal machine gun shot her back to the present.

"Our Stephen's got a girlfriend now, nothing serious though, too young for that, seems a nice girl, but you never know do you? Blonde, stays down Farm Road, father's a builder, nice car, Mercedes, bit flash, not brand new though, Tommy will be next, too quiet that's his problem, not that it's a problem, just you know, anyway, sure he'll find a nice girl, oh I got a text from that guy I met on Saturday, so he apologised for leaving like that, he had work in the morning, how he made it in his state I don't know, anyway he's buying me a drink later, I'll let you know how I get on, eh? Anyway, have to go, the gas man's coming to check the boiler, hell of a racket, so, you ok?"

"Fine, Margo."

"Ok. Good to have a wee chat, eh? See you tomorrow."

And away she went, the way she came, as Jean nodded off again, to somewhere quiet and painless.

CHAPTER 2

The school bell did its tired and clanky best to rally the troops as the entrance was breached, leaving Tommy and Stevie momentarily stripped of control, sucked into the chaotic flow of school life. Corridors became arteries, barely able to contain the turbulent teenage currents crashing and heaving with a volatile hormone cocktail of angst, indifference and lust.

Stevie made the most of the opportunity to run his fingertips over Sharon Perry's left buttock, barely concealed by the faintest hint of a skirt. Avoiding eye contact and any hint of a smile, he disappeared into the throng.

"Who the fuck...?" shouted the startled 17 year old, looking around for the culprit, a sign of guilt, someone to slap. But the moment was gone.

"Lovely!" he said grinning to his bemused friend.

"Eh?"

"Just copped a feel of Sharon Perry's arse."

"Pervert."

"Jealous?"

"Damn right." Tommy laughed. And jealous he was, not so much of a fleeting moment of eroticism, but of Stevie's generally carefree attitude to life.

As they pin-balled their way on and on through flailing body parts and pitiless doors, they finally came to room 37B and the white knuckle thrill of chemistry with Mr Richards.

"Another 2 hours of pish! Don't know why I bother coming. It's not like I'm going to be a chemist, or some mad scientist with a head the size of a fucking hippo!" moaned Stevie.

The reason was simple. He'd nothing else to do. No job, training or apprenticeship and no benefits. So with Margo's toe and even sharper tongue to propel him, here he was.

"I quite like it," countered Tommy

"Freak."

The classroom was a soulless box, with little in the way of decoration or distraction, just the odd poster and regulation periodic table blue tacked to peeling walls. Functional and cost effective in the eyes of accountants and administrators, but inspiring to neither teacher nor pupil. Mr Richards and his students grudgingly turned to face each other and got on with it. Tommy leaned forward and listened. Stevie leaned back, switched to survival mode and let all talk of combustion equations and polar bonding deflect safely off the armour of his indifference. Five minutes later he was asleep.

And sleep he did until awoken by the bell announcing the lesson was over. The class arose in unison and bolted for the door as if to eliminate any possibility of a change of heart. However, just as freedom was secured came the realisation that the next lesson would be every bit as anaesthetising as the one just past, a lesson never learned by the goldfish swimming round and round. As Stevie walked on, Tommy suddenly found his path blocked by a short, mousy haired girl. She smiled with just a hint of intrigue, but more than enough to seriously unnerve him.

"Hi."

"Eh...what?" Asked Tommy, trying to figure out what was coming next. He didn't have long to wait.

"Sharon wants to know if you want to go to Anne Young's party."

Tommy's reddening face suddenly turned sheet white as his mind froze in panic. He stood there, mute for an eternity of seconds.

"Emm... Who with?"

"Who do you think? Sharon of course."

Tommy stood silent again, desperately trying to find a way out. "I'll think about it," came the feeble response, made barely audible by a mouth bone dry and almost paralysed.

"Eh?...ok," replied an astonished Mary Smith. Sharon Perry, as well as being Stevie's rear of this or any other year, was widely regarded as the best looking girl in fifth year. Mary on the other hand was at best plain, a status magnified by the company she kept. She was used to being ignored and as time passed almost expected it. But Sharon! Bewildered, she wandered over to her waiting friend, not quite sure what to tell her.

Sharon was tall and slim, but with curves. The first girl in her class to "mature", she was always going to have the boys' attention, but she was also stunningly beautiful. Blonde, shoulder length hair, bright blue eyes, she was Barbie brought to life. But Sharon was no dim-witted bimbo. Academically, she was in the top 5% in all of her classes, but more than that, she was smart. So when Mary approached and tentatively passed on Tommy's reply, Sharon smiled. Mary, relieved but even more bewildered, asked what she was smiling at.

"He's just shy. That's one of the things I like about him. That and he's cute of course."

Mary's tension melted and she started giggling like...well, a schoolgirl, as they set off still laughing, to Mrs Carpenter and English. Shakespeare was never that funny.

Tommy and Stevie pushed back the way they had come.

"What did the Hobbit want?"

"Eh? Nothing," mumbled Tommy nervously.

"She must have wanted something. Is she after your body?" he mocked. "Come on, spill."

"Well if you must know..."

"I must, I must."

"Sharon Perry wants me to go to Anne's party."

Stevie performed an emergency stop, staring wide eyed and open mouthed at his friend, oblivious to the multiple body collision and tirade of abuse from behind. Disbelief turned to jealousy and then to rage. He had long lusted after Sharon, and been turned down more times than he could ever admit to.

"With you? You've got to be fucking kidding! Really, you're taking the piss."

"What do you mean, taking the piss? What's the matter with me? Have I got some deformity I don't know about?" Tommy looked over his shoulder. " Have I got a hump? A tail? That's it. A bit hairy donkey tail and double English. I'm doomed!"

"Very funny. Look I asked her out once and got a knock back. So how come she…"

"Listen to Tom fucking Cruise! Cruise missile more like, a nose like that."

"There's fuck all up with ma nose."

"One quick turn of yer head and somebody could lose an eye."

"Fuck off. So, when is it?"

"Don't know. You're going out with Anne, so you tell me."

"Na, I dumped her. She was getting too clingy, always wanting to come round. A man needs his space you know."

The truth of the matter was that Anne had grown tired of Stevie's hands trying to explore her underwear at every opportunity, and had dumped him two days earlier. At a week, this was Stevie's longest relationship and to his surprise he found himself slightly upset. He vowed never to let it happen again.

"Yeah, I know what you mean. I haven't made my mind up yet."

"Made up your mind about what?"

"Whether I'm going."

"Whether…. You've got to be kidding me! You've got to be fucking kidding me."

"Don't start that again."

"What's to think about? Are you a fucking bum boy or something?"

"Look, I'll probably go."

"Probably eh…Let's get the fuck out of here before this day gets any weirder, though that would probably involve time travel or fucking spacemen. Geez."

Tommy was vaguely aware of Mrs Carpenter moving around the class and sound coming from the vicinity of her head, but otherwise he was lost in his own work of fiction. Sorry tales and dramas. Boy meets girl. Boy doesn't have a clue what to say to girl. Boy tries to kiss girl but misses. Girl laughs at boy. Everyone laughs at boy. Boy runs out, can't go to school again because everyone will know and laugh and think he's an arse. No school, no qualifications, no university, no job, no life…Just because he went to Anne Young's bloody party! I could fall down the stairs and say I hurt my back…but maybe I'd break my neck…I wouldn't need to really fall, just make a lot of banging and falling down stair type noises, then lie down and moan or mybe …Tommy's panic was suddenly broken by Mrs Carpenters shrill yell.

"Tommy! Tommy! You be Oberon."

"Aye, king of the fairies, that's him," chirped Stevie.

As the class united in laughter, Tommy felt his face grow warmer and warmer.

"Nice beamer Tommy," yelled a voice from the back.

Tommy sighed and wished he were a time travelling spaceman.

CHAPTER 3

Normally, when Tommy got home from school he'd go straight into the living room, see how his mum was, say hello to his dad, make a cup of tea for them all and discuss each other's day. As his mother's condition worsened, Tommy became all too aware of the importance of this rare remaining source of pleasure. But this was not a normal day. Today Tommy went straight upstairs to his room and closed the door behind him. As he sat on the edge of his bed his mind raged in panic. Why did she have to ask him? Why could she not have just left him alone? But at the same time, he'd fantasised about this so many times, both in and out of the bathroom. He cursed his shyness as he desperately searched for a way out. He wished he could go through with it, but he couldn't. Could he? What was the problem? What was wrong with him?

"Tommy? Are you in, Son?" Yelled his father, Danny. "Tommy!"

"Yeah. I'm just upstairs!"

"Are you not coming in to talk to your mum?"

Tommy paused for a second. He hated lying to them, but he just wanted to be alone, to focus on his pain and self-pity.

"I'm not feeling well." He yelled back before hearing the stairs creak under his dad's weight. "Shit." He whispered.

The door opened and his father stepped into the room. Danny was a big man, 6 feet tall and built like a wrestler. Intimidating to those who didn't know him, but those who did knew his warm heart, reflected in an ever present smile.

"What's up then, Son?"

"Nothing Dad, I've just got a bit of a cold and I'm feeling really tired."

"Come on down and talk to your mum, you know how she is."

Tommy thought about another excuse, but didn't have the heart. He knew very well how she was.

"I'll even make the tea, Son, can't say fairer than that." His dad's smile broadened as Tommy rose from the bed.

As they entered the living room, Danny went into the kitchen to put the kettle on. Jean looked at her son and knew something wasn't right. "What's the matter, Son?"

"Eh, nothing, Mum. Just a bit of a cold. Think I'll have an early night."

"You sure, Son? You seem a bit worried."

Danny came back into the room as he waited for the kettle to boil. "Worried? What you worried about Son?"

"Nothing, I'm just a bit tired."

"Someone been picking on you at school?"

"No, Mum, nothing like that."

"So it is something then?"

"Come on Tommy you can tell us," his father said gently. "Maybe we can help."

"You can't."

"You're getting me worried now, Son, what is it?" asked his mother, her voice finding new strength.

"It's...nothing...look, a girl asked me out at school, that's all."

Parental tensions vanished as his parents shared a smile, and then went in for the kill.

"Who is she?" asked Mum.

"Do we know her?" enquired his grinning Dad.

"Do you like her?"

"What's her name?"

"Where are you taking her?"

"Stop! You're like the Spanish Inquisition! I don't even know if I'm going out with her yet."

"Do you like her?" enquired his mum, half smiling, half serious.

"Yes."

"Well then, what's to think about?"

"It's just that I...it's not that simple."

"It is Son." Said his dad, his voice soothing but firm. "Look I know you're shy and you think you'll make a fool of yourself and blah blah blah, but everyone has a first date, everyone's nervous, I know I was. I'm sure your girlfriend will be too."

Tommy was surprised. He actually felt his dad understood, though the blah's weren't too helpful. Maybe Sharon would be just as nervous. And he did like the sound of "your girlfriend". Tommy smiled for the first time since the invite.

"Kettle's boiled."

CHAPTER 4

The fading sunlight was seamlessly replaced by the orange glow of streetlights, as Tommy approached Sharon's front door. To anyone else, the house was unremarkable at best. Grey roughcast walls, recently double glazed by a newly energy efficient council. Its front door was stained mahogany with a brass handle and knocker, the remnants of DIY up marketing, now weathered and tarnished. Humble enough, but to Tommy this was a palace of demons. The door he was about to knock could be the entrance to every fear he had ever imagined, and no doubt a few he hadn't. But yet, if he pulled it off, just maybe it could be the realisation of all his fantasies. Sharon Perry, his girlfriend.

He felt sick with dread as he readied himself to knock on the door, to spin the wheel with heaven or hell to play for. He swallowed hard, dried the palms of his hands against his trousers, paused, and then knocked. He waited...and waited. Nothing. He felt his anxiety spike and knocked again. Again no reply. It was all a joke after all. She was just having him on. After all why would she want to go out with him? The whole school would be in on the joke. But then, mercy. "Can someone get the door?" he heard Sharon shout from inside.

A moment later the door opened to reveal Sharon in miniature. She smiled for a moment, sensing his nervousness with the mixture of innocence and evil only found in the young female of the species.

"What?" she asked, now frowning.

"Ehhmm, eh."

"You're not Eminem! Who you looking for?!" she barked, knowing only too well.

"Eh, is Sharon in?"

The girl stared up at him frowning intensely, maintaining the tension until, just when Tommy felt on the verge of complete collapse, the girl smiled, turned and ran inside. "Sharon! It's your boyfriend!" she screamed with glee.

A reddening Tommy stood at the now open door, aware of curtains moving and eyes staring.

"Shut up dwarf!"

Sharon slowly descended the stairs, coming into view piece by perfect piece. Black high heels, tanned legs, more leg, still more leg halted at the gates of indecency by the shortest of skirts, before flesh was bared once more, navel, white crop top, then finally her face, a face he'd seen a hundred times in his dewy eyed, heart racing, happy ending, teenage imaginings. She smiled at him and he melted.

"Hi," she said, with no hint of nerves.
Tommy just smiled.

"Let's go then," she gently commanded, taking his hand and leading him away.

"You look nice," he whispered, smiling as his nerves eased.

"Just nice?" she replied in mock indignation.

"Ok, beautiful."

"Just beautiful?"

He smiled and squeezed her hand. Maybe it was going to be a good night after all.

CHAPTER 5

Anne Young's home was as ostentatious as Sharon's was humble. It was built by Anne's builder dad on a 2 acre plot, on the outskirts of Sandyhill. It was also built by Anne's builder dad to let everyone know that he had money. Lots of money. He had made something of his life. He had succeeded where all those snobby cunts that had treated him like a moron at school had failed. A 6 bed roomed, sandstone, triple garaged, mock Greco columned, wrought iron-gated fuck you to the class of '85.

Tommy pushed the doorbell and smiled as Beethoven's 5th rang out.

"Classy," whispered Tommy.

Sharon shushed him as someone approached, unable to hide her own amusement.

Anne Young opened the door to her two smiling guests, dressed from head to toe in black leather.

"What are you smi....oh, the bell. Classy, eh?" She smiled, well aware of her father's taste issues.

"Go on into the living room. Nearly everyone's here, so you're almost fashionably late. Did you bring any drink?"

"Eh, no," mumbled Tommy shamefaced.

"Yes," beamed Sharon, pulling a bottle of vodka from her handbag.

"Wow, nice one...how did you get it?"

"Big brothers are a pain, but they have their uses."

"Brilliant!" exclaimed Anne holding the trophy aloft. "Alan, Chas and Stevie managed to get some booze, and I nicked some whiskey and wine that Dad won't miss, so that should get things going," she winked, as they went into the living room.

"Stevie?" asked Tommy quizzically. "He didn't say he was coming. I thought you had split up?"

"He just turned up with a big bag of beer and two bottles of wine. You don't tell Santa Claus to fuck off," Anne replied pragmatically, every bit the builder's daughter.

Tommy was glad to see his friend, to have someone else to talk to, but he also knew Stevie, and that made him more than a little uncomfortable. While Sharon and Anne headed into the kitchen to pour out some drinks, he made his way over to the other side of the spacious, dazzlingly white living room.

"You didn't say you were coming."

"Just thought I'd keep a protective eye on you in case Sharon's intentions are less than honourable."

"I'll take my chances."

"You want one of these?" Offered Stevie, holding out a can of Stella.

Tommy hesitated. He knew his parents would be upset if he went home drunk, but he also knew he'd be seen as a joke if he said no.

"Cheers." If he spread his drinks over the night, he could give the impression of joining in but not give the game away when he got home. "Some place, eh?"

"Yeah, massive," replied Stevie. "Can't see it staying the same colour, though."

Tommy looked around at the white walls, carpet and leather suite, nodding in agreement as he watched Alan Hunter's cigarette ash fall, the carpet turning blacker with every clumsy attempt to pick it up.

"No chance." Tommy took an exploratory sip from the can. Not only had he never been drunk, he had never tasted alcohol. Neither of his parents were big drinkers. A few on special occasions. On deciding he liked it, he took a gulp to rehydrate a mouth dried by nerves. "Where did you get them?"

"Big John."

Sharon made her way back to Tommy through the now bustling lounge, in each hands two glasses half filled with vodka and orange.

"There you go babe."
If hearing Sharon Perry call him babe didn't warm him enough, the generously measured vodka finished the job. Taste wise, he didn't like it as much as the beer, but the orange did enough to make it palatable. He took another gulp and smiled at his girlfriend.

"Nice, just the way I like it."

As the lights dimmed and the music grew louder, she took his hand.

"Let's dance."

Nearly spilling his drinks as he was jerked into the middle of the room, he quickly gulped down the vodka and put the glass down on a glass topped coffee table, pushed over to the side of the room to create a makeshift dance floor complete with mirror ball hanging from the ceiling. Tommy hated dancing probably more than anything else in the world, with the possible exceptions of speaking at the front of the class and giving Stevie's mother a kiss at New Year. He watched those around him and tried his best to copy them, keeping his movements as low key as possible. Sharon looked disapprovingly at the can of beer in his hand.

"You should have left that next to mine. Watch you don't spill it."

"It'll be fine, I'll empty it a bit." Tommy took a couple of large gulps. "Good party, eh?" He grinned, tension loosening its grip.

"Glad you came now?" she asked, almost accusingly.

"Yeah. It wasn't you I wasn't sure about, it was…just…" As his anxiety began to resurface, she smirked and let him off the hook.

"I know, I know, I'm just winding you up."

Composure regained, his confidence and dance moves grew in equal measure. He was having a great time. No doubt about it. Even the music, chart stuff he and his fellow music snob Stevie would normally despise, seemed fun. 'Now That's What I Call Music Volume 643 with a bit of old-school rave to keep the party bouncing. All his fears seemed distant and ridiculous. He looked over at Stevie, confident and charismatic. Even those who said they couldn't stand him thought warmly of him in their guilty secret moments. But tonight he felt his equal. Even on top for once. He took another mouthful of beer and turned the dance moves up a notch.

Stevie sat on the arm of a chair nursing a bottle of red wine. In between gulps he would slowly let the bottle tilt just enough to spill a few drops on the very expensive and impractical carpet, smug in the secret knowledge of the rage to come. Bob the Builder had a reputation which Stevie had no wish to experience first-hand. No, Bob and Angie Young's ETA was 2 am, so Stevie would exit 1.30, latest. He looked at his watch: 10 O'clock. Stifling a yawn, he looked around the room with a contemptuous glare and made his way to the bathroom upstairs. Closing the door behind him, he turned to see himself surrounded by his own image reflected in mirrored tiles stretching from floor to ceiling. He unzipped his fly and watched himself take a piss, dick in one hand, bottle in the other, making a hell of a mess as he turned to sample the view. Smiling at the madness of it. On a shelf in front of him were the usual toiletries, shaving gear, and some expensive looking porcelain figurines. Swaying slightly, he steadied himself by holding onto the window latch. Seeing an opportunity for entertainment, he opened the window, and began nudging selected items one at a time out the window, his mood lightening with every tinkle from below. Suddenly his playtime was interrupted by some frantic banging on the door.

"Will you be long?!" asked a girl's voice, in obvious distress.

"Maybe."

"Hurry up, I'm bursting."

"Is there not another one? A place this size, there must be."

"They're full! Hurry up will you."

Stevie took another swig and opened the door.

"Entrance fee, one kiss."

"In your dreams, arsehole," spat Mandy Peters, a big girl with a small sense of humour.

"Can I watch then?" asked Stevie.

"Watch this!"

Stevie ducked, but not quickly enough, a deodorant can glancing off his head before hitting the wall, cracking one tile from end to end.

"Fuck" they both gasped, before bolting for the door.

"Not a word" hissed Mandy, momentarily distracted from her bulging bladder by the thought of Bob's fury as they rushed downstairs.

As the time passed, Stevie dripped the final dregs of wine on the carpet, growing bored. Looking around, he caught Tommy's eye, who by this time thought he was giving Michael Jackson a run for his money. He raised his hand holding an invisible beer, signalling the need for more dance fuel. Stevie gave him the thumbs up, leaning over to take a couple of cans from the carrier bag he'd hidden, before making a detour to the kitchen where he found a few lost souls sitting around the kitchen table having a cosy old chat. Ignoring attempts to engage, Stevie made a beeline for the half full bottle of vodka in the corner. Cracking open the two cans of beer, he took a long gulp from one, then topped it up with vodka. "This will get you moon-walking Tommy."

Re-entering the living room, he made his way over to Tommy, making sure to brush firmly against Sharon, but with both hands in the air to maintain his innocence.

"There you go mate. Cheers."

Cans clinked, Sharon glowered and Stevie retreated, looking around for a drunken damsel in need of a helping hand.

As the room grew dense with thudding bass drum and cigarette smoke, Sharon pulled Tommy close to her, one hand round his waist, the other behind his neck.

"Go easy with that," she whispered, biting his earlobe gently.

"I'm fine, I've not had that much. I'm just having a good time. I'll just have another one or two." With that he sucked down half the can.

"Let's sit down for a while and talk," said Sharon, once again taking him by the hand and pulling him over towards an empty corner. He swayed behind her until they came to a halt and sat down heavily, propped up by the wall. Gulping down the remainder of the cans secret cargo, he crumpled the can, discarding it with cartoon machismo on the carpet.

"Magic!"

Sharon shook her head with a rueful smile.

"So what you want to talk about babe?"

"Nothing in particular. You. I see you at school every day. I like you, but I don't really know the first thing about you."

"A man of mystery, that's me. What do you want to know?"

"What do you like to do, what are you interested in? The usual things. What music do you like, for starters?"

"Old stuff. Motown, the Beatles, the Stones. What about you?"

"Lots of different things. What about Chart stuff?"

"Na, it's a bit girly."

"Well I am a girl, in case you hadn't noticed."

"Now you mention it." He smiled, putting his hand on her knee, leaning over to kiss her.

"Not here. Let's go upstairs."

As they departed, Stevie embarked on another kitchen refuelling mission, re-emerging with two glasses. One for him and one for the clearly worse for wear Mandy Peters, or Manky Mandy as she was secretly known, as much for her cavalier attitude to personal hygiene as her alleged minimalist morality. But for all the talk he didn't know of anyone who'd got one leg over the gate, never mind munched the meadow. He looked over at her, slumped over the arm of the couch having a staring contest with the carpet which, from her deep frown, she appeared to be losing. He smiled with Machiavellian confidence and swaggered over, sitting down on the carpet next to her. She lay like a dying beached whale, head limp, eyes opening and closing, trying to focus, to make sense of the situation, before deciding she wanted no part of it. Stevie, on the other hand, had other ideas, but seeing his evening about to go quite literally down the toilet, his mind set to work. He quickly looked around the room for one last check of the options. These, he saw, were now pretty limited. His recent aversion to relationships eliminated him from the night's routine partnering up, which was now almost complete, with the unlucky and just plain ugly heading for an early exit. With this confirmed, he scanned the room once more, casting his eyes and disdain over the handholding, all grown-up Stepford men and wives that were his peers, checking that no one was paying attention to him or the object of his affection. As luck would have it, they only had eyes for each other.

"Wankers," he muttered to himself.

Back to the job in hand, Stevie moved to reposition himself between the crowd and his intentions, gently stroking Mandy's pale and clammy cheek. "You ok, Mandy?" He whispered. With no reply, he began to slide his finger slowly from her cheek to her neck, staying there for a minute. As he reached the first button on her blouse, he felt his heart begin to pound, egging him on to go further. He unfastened a button and then a second button and let his right index finger continue its clandestine journey down to the first soft touch of breast, lightly coated in perspiration, then further, moving slowly and lightly across her right breast before coming to a stop at some strategically placed tissue paper. Fat with small tits. God can be cruel, he thought to himself. Undeterred, he pushed onwards and downwards until he reached her nipple, as soft, flaccid and lifeless as its owner. Turning back to the party, he half expecting to see a row of staring eyes and dropped jaws, but his luck was still holding. However, he knew it wouldn't last and as he turned back to face Miss Right Now, he also knew this wasn't enough. They had to find somewhere they could be alone together for some private time. Unfortunately however, for this to happen she would need to be awake or at least semi-conscious. He began lightly slapping her cheek.

"Mandy. ...Mandy, let's get you somewhere more comfortable. Mandy, wake up, you can't stay here, you can't be comfortable sitting like that."

As he began slapping her more forcefully her eyes squinted open.

"That's it Mandy, good girl. Up you get."

"What time is it?" she mumbled though debris encrusted lips.

"Oh it's early yet, plenty of time, you just need a quick lie down to clear your head."

He shoved his left hand under her head and lifted, but the dead weight attached was going nowhere. He sighed deeply as he stared defeat in the face. How the fuck was he going to get Mandy Peters, tiny tits and all, up the fucking stairs. Just when he'd resigned himself to an evening of clandestine flesh raiding, in a flash he had it. He jumped up, but not too quickly as to draw attention and made his way nonchalantly to the kitchen which was by now empty, all the losers having left. Finding what he was looking for, he made his way back, making sure to avoid eye contact before taking his position and putting his master plan into operation.

"Maaannddyyyyy," he whispered in her ear. "Maaaanndyyy, wake uuup." He began slapping her cheek again, more and more firmly. Her eyes opened to slits as she hovered around consciousness. With that, he slipped the glass of cheap whiskey under her nose. "Doesn't that smell nice?" The briefest of inhalations and its work was done. Suddenly her eyes opened wide.

"I'm going to be sick," she gagged.

"Well let's get you up to the toilet then. Quick now, you don't want to make a mess of this nice white carpet do you?"

Meanwhile, upstairs, Sharon and Tommy sat on the edge of the bed wondering what to do next. Tommy's heart raced in the moonlit semi darkness with a mixture of amazement at his good fortune, and terror at what he'd gotten himself into. Sharon, feeling vulnerable at having taken the lead, if not quite dragging him upstairs, waited for her uncertain partner to make the next move. Both were temporarily struck dumb for what seemed like a trembling, tension-filled eternity until Tommy broke the silence out of sheer panic.

"It's big, isn't it?" Tommy spluttered, surveying the king size, black silk-sheeted bed.

"I don't know, I haven't seen it yet," she joked, the tremor in her voice betraying her own nervousness.

With all doubt about what was expected removed, he put his arm round her, half excited, half condemned man, stumbling fearfully into the unknown. As their lips met, he felt her tongue inside his mouth, gently caressing. He followed suit, duplicating her every move. Leaning back, she pulled him down beside her as they sank deep into the soft quilt beneath them. She took his hand and placed it on her abdomen, giving him the signal that it was ok, leaving the detail up to him. He headed north, sliding his hand beneath her top and over her bra, his breathing growing heavier. She leaned forward to help as he moved his trembling hand around, clumsily trying to unfasten the clasp, before taking pity on him.

"It's a bit tight," she lied, snapping it open with ease.

Now inside his adversary, he began gently squeezing her breast, unable to believe what was happening as he turned his attention to the firm nipple, first stroking, then twisting.

"Gently, you're not looking for Radio One."

"Sorry," he whispered, suddenly flustered by his apparent failure.

"It's ok," she whispered, her reassuring smile unnoticed in the darkness as she pushed her tongue in his ear.

Not wanting to repeat his mistake, he removed his hand and headed south, briefly stroking her thigh almost as a courtesy before slipping his hand around under her skirt, placing it tentatively on her behind, ready to apologise, waiting for the slap....which never came. As he squeezed firmly, he felt he'd been given the keys to the kingdom. Gasping, hearts pounding, lips and tongues dancing, suddenly all reservations disappeared as he began to explore with feverish abandon, first playing with what remained of her pubic hair, before her parting thighs invited him through heaven's gates to the earthly delights inside.

Although he had seen pictures of female genitalia, the exact location and function of all its parts were a mystery. As he stumbled around blindly in her underwear, Sharon slid her left hand down to the front of his trousers, moving first slowly, then faster, pressing harder, unsure of whether it was having the desired effect or indeed any effect at all. Deciding there was only one way to find out, she pulled down the zip and after a few seconds found the opening in his boxers. As Sharon began her own exploration, Tommy found himself torn from the dream like bliss of carefree sensual indulgence, to the reality of pleasure tainted by expectation. As he tried to gauge the effects of her efforts for himself, her next words confirmed the worst. "Is everything OK?"

Tommy felt his world unravel as he tried to arouse himself by shear strength of will. Beads of sweat broke out on his forehead as he cursed himself for drinking so much, blowing the biggest opportunity of his short life. His mouth dried and his heart raced even faster as desperation threatened to overwhelm him. Then, just before desperation turned to despair. Just before the dreaded lie that it didn't matter, when right now it mattered more than anything in the world, salvation appeared from the strangest quarter. Suddenly the bedroom door burst open, the light dazzling the nocturnal lovers as they sat bolt upright, hurriedly adjusting their clothes. Still blind, they heard a familiar voice bellow from the hall.

"Not in there, Mandy."

But it was too late. As Tommy and Sharon squinted through the glare, Mandy retched from the depths, hurling her tepid payload straight in the face of the startled Sharon. Unfortunately, the nature of the startle reflex is such that on most occasions it's coupled with an involuntary opening of the mouth. While this can be useful on some occasions, this wasn't one of them, and as the stream of lumpy alcohol ran down her mouth and throat, her reflexes changed quickly from startle to gag as she to decanted her own stomach contents into her lap. As mind and body settled, she looked down and surveyed the wreckage of a body lusted after just moments earlier. Shrieks of hysteria quickly gave way to fury and recrimination.

"Look what you've done, you stupid fucking bitch!"

Sensing that her words were wasted on a Mandy Peters by now on her knees and oblivious to time and space, she turned her attention from this pitiful wreck to her apparent accomplice.

"I might have known you'd be involved you weasel faced little prick."

"What did I do?" Stevie protested tensely, fully grasping the ramifications of even the faintest hint of a smile.

Unfortunately it would appear his efforts were inadequate.

"Get born!" she screamed lurching to her feet, wine bottle in hand.

Fortunately for Stevie, as she stood up, the contents of the punch bowl formed in her lap spilled its nauseating contents down once sexy legs, dissolving her violent rage into pitiful humiliation.

"Just fuck off!" she screamed, rushing past him into the hall.

"Sharon, wait!" yelled Tommy.

He jumped up off the bed before tripping quickly back down to earth, or more accurately on top of the now prostrate and unconscious Mandy. Now it is an inescapable fact of life that no matter how bad things are, they can always get worse, and just as Tommy was trying to get back to his feet, unintentionally using Mandy's partially exposed and extremely slippery breasts for leverage, Mary Smith unlocked the bathroom door to investigate the screams of her best friend. Her face froze in disbelief at the sight of a writhing Tommy groping the comatose girl beneath.

"You dirty bastard!" roared Mary the mouse. "You dirty fucking bastard!" She turned and raced off to find her friend.

By now the curiosity of even the most absorbed of downstairs hand-holders was gripped by the screams of the two girls now fleeing the premises and they scurried up the stairs to investigate. The sight of Tommy, now on his knees and zipping up his trousers as he straddled Mandy's face, stopped them in their tracks. Then, as if to prove the earlier stated fact beyond any naïve doubt, Mandy's eyelids, flickering for a second, jerked wide open as she stared at the crotch, zipper in hand just inches from her face. As her screams pierced the stunned silence, she brought her fist hard against her assailant's groin before shoving him aside and scrambling to her feet.

"Fucking perv bastard!"

With Tommy's descent into British theatrical farce complete, Stevie, sensing the potential gravity of the situation, ducked back into the bedroom to avoid guilt by association. He watched as his friend was grabbed by the pack and shoved against the wall, his denials of wrong doing having as much success as a rent boy in a convent. Peering from the darkness he saw his friends face become more desperate. He also knew he would be dragged into it eventually, so better now before police involvement escalated things.

31

"Wait! Leave him alone, he didn't do anything."

As the mob quickly turned its attention to him, Stevie paused to gather his thoughts. After relaying the events, missing out his part in Mandy's unfortunate condition, the anger began to dissipate. But just as Tommy began to feel relief, the accusations and threats were slowly replaced by laughter, quietly at first, but with increasing fervour and cruelty. It was now Tommy's turn to hurriedly exit stage left, tears welling in his dimmed, despondent eyes. Concluding he'd want to be on his own for a bit, Stevie stood soberly as the crowd dispersed back downstairs. He turned to Mandy standing in the corner, head down leaning against the wall as the effects of the adrenaline wore off. "You ok, Mandy?"

"Tired," he mumbled.

"Tired? Well then...let's get you home, eh?"

CHAPTER 6

The stars twinkled mockingly in their heavens as Tommy walked the friendless, desolate road home. The streets were empty, dim and silent, as if everyone knew, desperate to shun the loser of losers. The late evening chill added to the sense of numbness he felt. Suddenly a wave of nausea hit him and he opened his mouth, watching as a stream of alcohol and bile projected several feet in front of him, never missing a step. As he approached his front door he paused briefly to reflect on dealing with his parents, but only briefly. He didn't care. Opening the door, he stepped inside and immediately his Dad was in front of him.

"How did it go then?" he asked, bursting with curiosity.

"I'm going to bed."

Taking one look at the heartbreak in his son's eyes, he moved to the side, allowing him to pass silently, to climb the stairs as many a condemned or broken hearted man had before him. He sat on the side of his bed, head in hands, mourning his loss, eyes squinting around the moonlit room seeking comfort in familiarity, but finding none. He undressed and slid under the covers, resting his head, closing his weary eyes in search of peace but finding only disorientation as the room began to spin beneath him. He opened his eyes quickly, stopping the tailspin momentarily, but even that wasn't enough, only taking the edge off

33

as a fresh wave of nausea washed over him. He sat up quickly, too quickly, trying to think. The toilet? Too far. He looked over at the moonlights silvery glow, but this was not the time for admiring the view. He swung his legs across the bed, mouth clamped tightly shut and leapt to the window, opening it just in time as the last fiery dregs were ejected through this nose to the street below. He fell back onto the bed, hoping it was over but... with no time he surrendered, retching uncontrollably, his now empty stomach offering only pain. He closed his eyes, opened his eyes and stared at the ceiling, desperately trying to cling to something solid. Then the silence ended, and the thoughts flooded in, chastising, mocking, guilt ridden, drowning in anxiety at the humiliation to come, pointing, sniggering, questioning. Then the tears, gently at first, then uncontrollable floods. He turned, buried his face in the pillow and wished that he were dead.

The next morning Tommy awoke, groggily at first, then sharply, stabbed by the realisation of what had gone on. Dread's cold sweat enveloped him as he imagined his fate. There was also the real and present sickness ravaging his whole body. This was why Anne's parents allowed the party on a school night. The perfect revenge for those on whom warnings had failed. Tommy imagined them, surveying the carpet, smiling. Smiling, because for each stain there was a white faced, red eyed little arsehole praying for their sickness to stop, promising abstinence for all eternity in return. Worth the price of cleaning.

Genius. Bastards! He looked at the alarm clock. 6 am. Early, no doubt awoken by subconscious terror. He could stay off sick. Which would be true, self-inflicted, but true none the less. He also knew that if he didn't go, get it over with, it would just spin round and round in his head, leaving him an emotional wreck. He had to get it done. It also allowed him to nip the more salacious gossip in the bud. He'd just have to tough it out. He suddenly realised that in all his self-pity, he'd never thought once about Sharon. Maybe last night just confirmed what he knew all along. That he didn't deserve her. She was out of his league and would now treat him with the distain he'd always assumed, before their little detour through the looking glass. What had he been thinking?

Tommy checked the clock every 5 minutes as he imagined every possible embarrassment. On the one hand, wishing he could just get on with it, on the other, trying to stop time. Then suddenly, with one giant leap forward it was 8am. Time to get up. To face...5 more minutes...and another. At 8.23, he swung his legs to the side of the bed, slowly this time. Resignedly he put on the clothes his mother had laid out the evening before. He washed, cleaned his teeth, looking accusingly at the reflection in the mirror. Not for the first time, he wished he was Stevie and just didn't give a fuck. "This is another fine mess you've gotten me into," he whispered. He slowly descended into the kitchen where his breakfast sat on the table. On either side his parents briefly looked up then back down, not sure what to say, so saying nothing, preferring an awkward silence to awkward questions and even more awkward answers. Ten minutes later he got up, put on his coat and left before Stevie knocked on his door.

The morning chill felt good, clearing the fuzziness as he picked up pace to meet the enemy ahead. As he reached the end of the street he sensed Stevie behind. "And so it begins," he muttered under his breath. He stopped, allowing his smiling friend to catch up. As he did, Stevie's smile seemed to get bigger and bigger. It was cartoonesque by the time he reached him. Tommy recoiled as Stevie marched straight at him.

Smell these!"

Tommy was taken aback as Stevie's fingers were suddenly thrust against his nose.

"Smell!" barked Stevie, manically.

Tommy took a quick sniff of the pungent but mysterious odour. He stared blankly at Stevie.

"Mandy Peters!" exclaimed Stevie, beaming with pride.

"Mandy Peters? But she was...unbelievable. Even for you. Have you not washed your hands since last night!?"

"Washed my hands? No way! I'll be wrapping these bad boys in cling film."

"You're a degenerate."

"I'm a degenerate? At least I didn't try and stick my dick in her face."

Tommy's face quickly reddened. "Don't start. I fell, you saw me."

"Yeah. Fell....dick first, right in her face."

Even Tommy had to laugh as they set off towards school. "What a disaster."

"Speak for yourself, " grinned Stevie proudly as he enjoyed the scent of his ill-gotten gains one more time.

Tommy's raised spirits soon began their sickening descent as the school building came into view, anxiety's grip tightening with every step. His face paled as he approached the gates, thoughts turning to flight.

"You ok?" Enquired Stevie. "You're not saying much."

"I'm fine," came the unconvincing reply.

"You look a bit pale."

"I'm fine!" He paused briefly, before opening the heavy door into the unknown. His first class was double Maths, which was close by, so he would have to parade the halls no longer than necessary. Unfortunately once there he would once again be sharing a room with Sharon. He held his breath and opened the door, stepping nervously into the class.

"Look out it's the sex fiend," chirped a voice from the other side of the class.

This was a cue for some half-hearted abuse and laughter, but fortunately for Tommy those who had been at the party were more concerned with their own fragile state. Most could barely lift their heads off the desk; their stomachs in no condition to feast on the banquet of cruelty Tommy had offered them on a plate.

Sitting down beside Stevie, he couldn't believe his luck. He'd thought his friend would have been unable to resist taking the piss, his favourite pastime after all. But on this occasion he may have opened himself up to some questions better left silent, a strategy made easier by Mandy Peters absence due to a "stomach bug." Tommy sat back in his chair and relaxed for the first time since the party...and then the door opened once more. Tommy watched as Sharon entered, gliding regally into the classroom with all the grace of a prima ballerina, her appearance immaculate as ever. She paused momentarily, looking around for an available seat. Tommy watched as she headed towards the empty desk in front of him. He scanned her expression. Calm, almost serene. Looking for a sign, he noticed the faintest hint of a smile and reciprocated. She understood. It wasn't his fault. She'd forgiven him. As she sat down, his smile widened.

"Hi." he whispered.

"Fuck off."

CHAPTER 7

Danny and Jean winced as the upstairs door slammed shut, surprised that such a level of volume could be generated by a 14 year old girl, and over such a seemingly trivial matter. They looked at each other, eyebrows raised. "They should ban parties," Danny muttered, sinking back into his chair.

However, for Susie Slater the matter of how long, or short to be more accurate, a skirt she could wear to Michelle's party was no trivial matter. But they didn't understand that. How could they? They were too old. They just sat and watched boring crap on television all night. How sad is that? They don't care what they wear, sitting about in old cardigans, or corduroy trousers or some other skanky old persons gear, because no one would see them anyway. But just because their life was over didn't give them the right to ruin hers. Why would they do that? Why would someone who supposedly loves you do that? Just deliberately ruin your life like that. Embarrass you to death in front of your friends. Why? Because they were just old and jealous, that's why.

She lay back on her bed and gazed around at the pictures on her wall. Pictures of pretty boy stars of the day stared back as they had for generations of girls. Girls angry with their parents. She was supposed to be going out with Luke at the party and there was no way she was meeting the coolest guy in class dressed as a librarian. She would just have to think of a plan. She lay for a while, thoughts drifting between plans and Luke.

The ring of the doorbell distracted her for a moment, as she listened to find out who it was.

"Hi Mr Slater, is Tommy in?"

She instantly recognised the voice as Stevie's, and smiled. She liked Stevie. Her mum and dad weren't too sure. But she was. He didn't treat her like a kid and he made her laugh. Not boring like some of her brother's other friends. Or her brother for that matter. She could never quite figure out how they'd ended up together. Total opposites. Stevie seemed far too exciting for her brother. Good looking, too.

"He's just popped out to the shop for milk. He'll be back in a minute, if you want to go upstairs and wait in his room."

"Ok, thanks."

Susie leapt to her feet and ran to the mirror, adjusting her hair as best she could, but time was not on her side. She would do. Then, just as Stevie reached the top of the stairs, Susie appeared in front of him. Head tilted to one side, she played with her hair and smiled, bright blue eyes gazing up, enjoying this strange new world.

"Hi, Stevie."

"Susie Q, how do you do," he answered, smiling back at her childish flirtation.

Maybe she had a little crush, but no harm in that. As an only child, Stevie had never experienced that sibling bond. Throw in the lack of a father, or a known one at any rate, the obvious fact he'd been an accident, albeit a loved one, it all added to the deep hole in his life where a "proper" family should be. But Susie felt more like his little sister with every year that passed. It was the same with Tommy. He knew people couldn't understand how they could be friends. And he could see why. On the surface they had little in common, but he knew they gave each other a little of what was missing in themselves. Associating with someone as intelligent as Tommy would maybe help him be taken a bit more seriously when his ego required it, a contender, not just a bum. Tommy on the other hand gained some street credibility from their association, and the chance to take a few tentative steps on the wild side when the mood took him. But there was a deeper side to it. More than anything he admired Tommy's goodness, because he knew it was the real thing. Not a façade to garner the admiration of respectable society fakers. Not just politeness. Not just good manners, which he had in abundance. No, Tommy was genuinely decent, something he knew he wasn't, but as long as Tommy saw something in him he had hope. They also liked each other, which everyone else seemed to miss.

"Do you want to wait in my room till Tommy gets back?"

"Ok gorgeous, but no rough stuff."

Susie blushed, giggling, slapping him on the arm.

"Better watch your boyfriend doesn't find out. He's not in there is he?"

She giggled again, much to her annoyance, worried Stevie would think she was just a silly little girl.

"Don't get me started about boyfriends."

"Susie Q, don't tell me you're going to break my heart now?"

As they sat down, Susie proceeded to tell her tale of woe. Stevie nodded sympathetically in the right places, partially listening, mainly enjoying the closeness he now felt. When she had finished he gave her a hug. "We'll think of something," he whispered.

But she already had. It had come to her as soon as she had heard his voice at the door. "Your mum could buy a dress for me."

If one thing was for certain, it was that Margo McDaid didn't do librarian. But there was always the risk of Margo going too far, leaving Suzie looking like a Bangkok hooker on a hen night. But a risk worth taking.

"I could get changed at your house."

"I don't know. She'd feel a bit awkward going behind your mum's back."

But he knew that Margo also doted on Susie. The combination of seeing little Susie growing up and some girly mischief would be too much to resist.

"Yeah, she'll do it."

"Hi, Stevie."

Startled, Stevie and Susie turned towards the voice, a hint of guilt lingering.

"What are you two up to?"

"Nothing, just chatting. I didn't hear you come in. See you later Susie."

"Yeah, later," she smiled.

They headed to Tommy's room and closed the door.

"You still on for Ian's tonight?" Stevie asked.

"Eh. I don't know. Mum and Dad are going out and I really need to stay in for Susie."

"Bollocks, Susie will be fine; she'll love having the run of the place. You want me to ask her?"

"No."

"Don't be bottling out."

"I'm not."

"Ian's got the acid, so...."

"Right, ok, fine."

"You sure?"

"I just said so."

"Ok, cool."

CHAPTER 8

James Paterson sat at his desk, in his office, in his bank with a radiant air of serenity. A half smile lifted the corners of his mouth as he gazed adoringly at the computer screen in front of him, sitting motionless as Mozart played almost inaudibly from a small radio sitting on a female colleague's desk in the main office. Almost five minutes passed before James moved, scratching the left hand side of his nose.

James had worked for the bank almost 22 years, exactly half his life, joining straight from university clutching degrees and fervent ambition in equal measure. Now a Branch manager, the plans he had made all those years ago were pretty much on track. Just to the left of his computer sat a small informal photograph of a petit middle-aged woman with black shoulder length hair, dressed in a red trouser suit. She was flanked by twin girls, blonde hair framing uncomfortable gazes, struggling to find a smile for the occasion. At their feet sat three dogs of indeterminate lineage.

James Paterson sat on and on, silent and still like a banker's Buddha. In his right hand was a Compaq three-button mouse; gripped securely, tight enough to turn James' knuckles white. Anne Smith left Mozart and the main office with a hand-full of white papers, which she deposited on Mr Paterson's desk without speaking. Now in her mid-thirties, Ms Smith was still an extremely attractive woman albeit in a stern, school mistress sort of a way, fresh faced, with short auburn hair and large Bambi-brown eyes. As she turned to leave, Mr Paterson wished he could drag her back, lift her on to his desk, slip her panties off over those oh so shapely hips and fuck her screaming, moaning, but fully consenting brains out!

James Paterson was probably more bored than he had ever been in his life. Bored!   Bored!!! Fucking BOOORRREEEEEEDDD!!!!!!!!!!!!!! He wanted to crush the fucking mouse to little tiny fucking bits and punch it through the reflection of the Homer Simpson tie that grinned out from the screen in front. "Today would be a good day to kill someone," he whispered to himself.

"Excuse me sir?"

"Nothing Anne, not a thing. You can go home now, have a good weekend, "he sighed.

"Thanks, you too. Don't work too late."

As she turned again to leave, he had one long last look, shaking his head wearily.

An hour later, James Paterson's metallic silver Lexus drove into the car park of the Black Duck pub on the outskirts of Sandyhill. A small, detached, very mock Tudor building surrounded by rundown wartime prefabs, it was well known as a haven for the green bottle, red nose brigade. It was a shit hole. But it was their shit hole. James had passed it every day for the last 7 years on his long commute home, but had never noticed it before tonight. He was only half an hour from the family home, but tonight he needed a drink and to be anywhere else. As he entered in his dark suit he looked like an undertaker at a pauper's funeral, a service most of the clientele looked as though they would be needing sooner rather than later. Men and women, young and old, they all shared gaunt eyes and ruddy complexions handed down through the generations. He walked through the damp sullen atmosphere straight to the bar.

"A large Brandy Alexander."

"I'm Tam. Alex only works the weekends," replied the stony faced barman, reaching for the Brandy bottle.

All eyes had been on James from the moment he walked through the door, like a change of channels in mid program, however normal service was gradually resumed. Over by the open fire four men played dominoes. Ranging in age between early twenties to about eighty, James noticed with bemusement that they all wore matching raincoats and flat caps which, even with the blazing fire, they all refused to remove. The bar's few other customers sat at separate tables; occasionally nodding to each other before returning their gaze to the half empty glasses in front of them, regularly checking their money for re-assurance it wasn't to be their last.

"Viva Las Vegas," muttered James under his breath, finishing the drink in one.

"Eh?" enquired the barman.

"Nothing. Another Brandy Tam," said James, with a slightly mocking tone.

"Coming up."

Suddenly the door burst open and a wild haired, wilder eyed man mountain lurched in, his blood-shot eyes darting around the room. "Yer just a shower o cunts, the lot o yeh!" He turned towards the black suit.

"And you. You. You're a cunting cunt!"

"Does he have Tourettes?" James whispered to the barman."

"No. He just thinks everyone's a cunt."

"Oh."

With his thick red hair and beard, he looked like a flaming torch as he staggered over towards the domino players, dropping onto a small wooden stool, which disappeared beneath his long tweed overcoat. He slumped forward, muttering, semi-conscious.

"Ffuu....cuuu..." Loud snoring soon followed, all ignored by the domino players. If it didn't have dots, it didn't exist. James looked at his watch. It was almost 8 o'clock.

"When does it get busy?"

The barman paused for a moment. "Saturday." James sighed and played with his drink. How the hell had it ever got to this, he thought to himself. As a schoolboy, James Paterson was at the top of the tree. Although academically bright, his real gifts lay in sport, particularly football. Captain of the school team, followed by girls and scouts in equal measure, he was Roy of the Rovers in the making. That was until a drunk driver launched him six feet in the air, leaving him with two shattered legs, before screaming off never to be

caught. Fifteen operations had got him walking again, but one solid tackle would put paid to that. So here he was all these years later, university, wife, 2 kids, bank managers job. His life summed up in eight words. He looked around. Yes, he had the suit, but he was no different from the rest of life's losers scattered around this turd-brown bar. But before his self-pity completely engulfed him, something caught his eye. At first he thought he was smoking while asleep. Strange enough, but that wasn't it. "He's on fire," he mumbled to no one in particular, before panic took hold. "He's on fucking fire!"
Captain Red Beard had fallen off his stool headfirst into the blazing log fire.

"Oh, that's just Hughie," replied the barman. "He's always falling in the fire."

Hughie slowly regained consciousness and his feet, swaying his way towards the bar, patting out the flames as he went. "Whi...whi...whiiiisky!" As the bartender duly obliged, James stood transfixed by the ginger mane and beard, still smouldering. Hughie turned to face him, taking his time to focus.

"Cunt!"

CHAPTER 9

STEVIE

Stevie fell onto the tired old couch next to Ian, having quickly learned the wisdom of always getting close to the man with the drugs, firstly to ensure he would get some, but also locating himself firmly up the subconscious pecking order. The man was...well, the man, but Stevie was happy to bathe in the reflected glory. Like the roadies on a tour, the groupies had to go through him to get to the star attraction. This evening, however, there were no groupies, no quiet desperation to get stoned, high, or be cool. Only three mates in a damp dingy room assured of getting what they wanted. The room décor was of a bygone age. Wallpaper, beige with nicotine played reluctant host to some original oil paintings, the work of Ian's father, an amateur artist with an unintentionally original technique. Great lumps of dazzling colour devoid of any recognisable form, but interesting...yes ...definitely interesting. Also on one wall hung a concave mirror distorting everything in its view, pining for it's rightful place in the hall of mirrors and all the fun of the fair. Ian had never figured out why his parents had hung it in their living room. Entertaining when drunk though.
Stevie looked over at Tommy.

"What's up T, you're looking a bit pale. Chickening out?”

"No. Just ...," his thought faded away.

"Right Ian, let's get this show on the road!"

"All in good time, let's get the vibe right. This is serious stuff. A 12 hour flight to destinations unknown. Best to get the pilot in a good mood, know what I mean."

Tommy shuffled in his seat nervously.

"Sure you're up for this Tommy? You look a bit tense there mate."

"I'm fine. Fine. Just ... fine."

"Just relax and let it wash over you. Don't try to control her, she won't like it," offered the grinning Ian.

Ian's reference to the drug in living terms increased Tommy's unease, but he couldn't back out now. The embarrassment of that would be worse than anything this stuff could throw at him, he reasoned. "Let's get on with it," he said solemnly, sitting upright in his chair.

"Well the man hath spoken Ian, let's be having it."

Ian smiled and reached into the frayed pocket of his favourite Oxfam shop jacket. A comfortable combination of Karma and style. He delicately pulled out a small square of silver paper from a pack of Marlboro's. The night's main event. He unfolded it and sat it on the table in front of them. For a moment they sat and looked, as if paying respects at the altar of some miniature deity. Ian reached out first, picking up one of the small pieces of blotting paper, putting it in his mouth and washing it down with a gulp of Buckfast tonic wine, kissing the bottle in appreciation. "Buckie", produced by Benedictine monks, was a potent mix of alcohol and caffeine which performed its sacred duty every weekend, fuelling staggeringly good times filled with love, hate, hugs and stabbings. Margo's tipple of choice from back in the day before emigrating South, she'd managed to track it down to a specialist shop and it had quickly found favour amongst Stevie's associates. But special as it was, tonight it was demoted to mere side order status.

"Who's next then?" he barked, offering the bottle to the next participant.

Stevie's grabbed the second dose, putting it on his tongue, looking down through crossed eyes, hesitating for a second, before grabbing the bottle and sending it on its way. He then looked over to Tommy who reached pensively for the remaining tab, picked it up and gazed warily, as if in a trance. He wondered what was going through his friend's head, but after a few moments impatiently thrust the bottle towards him. Tommy however, deep in his own thoughts didn't even notice, but eventually placed the chemical Eucharist reverentially onto his tongue. Epiphany or crucifixion, he wondered.
Stevie sat back, unsure of what to do next. How long before "it" happened. His outward bravado masked his own unease. Bluntly put, what would happen if he went nuts? Although he was no stranger to getting wrecked, no matter how out of control he seemed, he always felt he was pulling his own strings. Tonight, that might not be the case. Best to meet this stranger on home

turf. He reached over the side of the couch into his plastic bag and pulled out his own bottle of the monk's commotion potion. Twisting the screw top, he cursed his luck as the whole piece just rotated on the bottle top. A not uncommon occurrence. Monastic quality control left something to be desired.

"Bastard, a fucking twister," he moaned.

"Knifes in the kitchen," smiled Ian sympathetically.

After some frantic slashing at the joint between the cap and the supposedly stationary part, the seal was broken and the bottle held aloft in triumph. He took several gulps as if to make up lost ground.

"So when does this shit kick in then Ian, cos so far I'm feeling fuck all."

"Patience dear boy, let her wake up gently."

"Wake up gently? I think she's waiting for breakfast in bed!"

They both laughed, not knowing why or caring. Soon after, Stevie began to feel a tingling sensation run up his spine, spreading through his nervous system, through every atom, his teeth grinding, as a strange metallic taste filled his mouth. He sat back, relaxed and let it fill him. He hadn't been conned after all.

"Let's get some good music on!"

Lurching to his feet, he made his way to the scattered pile of CD's strewn across the pine shelf on the opposite wall. After some searching he found a suitable soundtrack to the evening. The stereo was old and battered, but loud, and it could play Hendrix. As Electric Ladyland filled the air in all its majesty, Stevie strapped on his invisible Stratocaster and played as if his life depended on it. With his teeth, behind his head, behind his back, he pulled out all the stops, oblivious to anything else. Ian applauded manically, pausing only for an up and down of the wine bottle. Just at that moment, Stevie, having leaned too far back mid solo, fell over the table, landing upside down in a heap at Ian's feet. Cue hysterical laughter, until eventually he managed to clamber back up onto the couch, sinking deep; it's long collapsed springs offering little in the way of resistance.

"I'm melting man," Stevie mumbled to everyone and no one.

"I'm a bit warm too." Tommy stuttered.

"Noooo man. I mean I'm really, really fucking melting man. I'm like...dissolving....like a big fucking smiley puddle...haaaahhaa."

Stevie and Ian erupted once more, huddled together, bonded in mad abandon, careless, carefree and who gives a fuck anyway.

"Enjoying it then?" asked Ian pointlessly.

"Na...its crap...haaaaahahaah."

Stevie leaned back and looked over at Tommy, who smiled back unconvincingly. He stared at Tommy's face, bright, shimmering, but isolated, separated by the vast intercontinental expanse of the coffee table. He was out, cast into the wilderness, outside looking in. Alone. All fucking alone, poor old Tommy. Poor old shiny, floppy haired, pure, angel Tommy stranded in one man's heaven, another man's hell. Which is it Tommy, eh? Which is it? Well I fucking know even if you don't. This is my world you've strayed into. You don't belong here, and don't you fucking know it...fuck it...fuck it...s'not your fault mate...but...haaahhaaahaa, man this is fucking nuts, he thought, his mind racing. He turned to Ian, who was constructing a cone, the behemoth of spliffs. The lighter exploded, sparkling intense heat, softening the hash, wisps of smoke, sweet smelling, pungent. Just then he felt another acid wave break over him. He knew which side of the table he was on, and heaven felt sweet. He sat beatifically; slowly waving his hands, black eyes following the tracers, mind absorbing the music which had come to life, filling the room, the world, his mind. A nudge diverted his attention to the flaming dope torch being passed, lighting the path to oblivion, he inhaled deeply, held the smoke deep in his chest...held it....held it, then release.

"ooooh mmmmaaan," He leaned back, transfixed. The smoke, now a living painting, so much detail, faces, eyes, smiling eyes, they understood, changing, growing, disappearing, reappearing...life...death, it was all right there. He reached out to grasp it, but couldn't...always slipping through his fingers. "You want some of this T?"

"Eh, no thanks, I'm fine," came the weak reply.

Stevie passed the spliff back to Ian, but his eyes remained on Tommy, now concerned for the first time.

"The smoke looks weird right enough"
pondered Ian. "I can see a man with a giant cock"
All concern disintegrated in laughter.

"Oh man...I'm on the fucking star ship
enterprise, hehehe," said Stevie, by now upside
down on the arm chair.

"Well, I've got a photon torpedo needs firing"
Replied Ian.

Left alone with Tommy, Stevie looked over and
studied his friend as David Attenborough would
a rare species of mammal. He looked so
bewildered and afraid. Stevie felt his fear radiate
out towards him and recoiled. Compassion
struggled with resentment. A friend in need is a
friend.... pissing on his parade. "Just relax mate,
go with it, it's just a laugh with your mates.
Nothing to worry about."

"Yeh, I am, I am." Tommy replied, more to
himself than his friend. With a forced smile, he
leaned back in the armchair. Just at that Ian
returned, trousers at his ankles. "Watch this," he
yelled, lifting the mirror from its hook, holding it
behind him, allowing the convex mirror to do its
trick. "Be honest. Does my arse look big in this?
Hahahahah. I tell you something, shitting on acid
is...just fucking weird. Like you're slowly turning
inside out, then you feel light as a feather, like
you could float up into the air."

"Make wiping your arse a bit tricky eh."

"I need a piss" muttered Tommy leaving the
room"

"A wank more like."

"Easy Ian, I think he's having a tough time," whispered Stevie.

"No fucking wonder, miserable bastard. Some can handle it, some cant. It just fucks with their head. He took the tab, he took the chance...anyway enough of his shit, open another bottle of wine, I'll stick some good sounds on."

As Stevie gulped, the opening chords of Street Fighting Man ripped through the room. Ian sat back down, leaning against him.

"The sound of gods made mortal, eh? Listen to that fucking guitar. Revolution in six strings, it's all there. No need for guns or bombs. That just cuts right through it all. Yer man Keef might have carried a gun or a blade from time to time, but those fucking chords just kill every fucking thing in their way. Like the grim reaper scything every bullshitting, lying, ego-tripping motherfucking politician, cop or cunt who gets in his way. That's the truth, right there. And Jagger never sounded better. Even he believed it. No fucking cartoon mockney rhyming slang bang thank you fucking maam. Even he saw how important it was. Know what I mean man? But Keef didn't even need to think about it, he just....was. Fucking great album. Before that they were just a good little beat group. But Beggars Banquet gets right to the guts of it. What a change, like their own little soul selling at the crossroads moment. Sympathy for the devil right enough."

"You got any beer?"

"Yeah, I'll get some." A few moments later Ian returned, arms laden but looking somewhat perplexed. "Where the fuck's Tommy?"

Stevie quickly swung right side up. "Is he not through there?"

"Not unless he's hiding down the pan, in which case he's having one motherfucking bad trip."

Stevie got up and they both had a look round.

"Tommy!...Tommy!" they both yelled.

Ian noticed the front door was open. "He's legged it."

"Fuck. We need to find him." Stevie bolted outside and looked around.

"He just needs to chill out, leave him be. He'll be fine in a few hours."

Stevie mulled it over. He'd been looking forward to this and so far he hadn't been disappointed. Tommy was probably tucked up in bed. A bit selfish of him, not saying anything, so why should he care. "Ye...probably in bed by now" muttered Stevie.

"Look up there…. a billion stars, just like us. Makes you feel small, eh?" Said Ian as if seeing them for the first time with the rapt attention of a new-born child. "Fancy going camping? I've got a tent. A night under the stars. Maybe pick up Weasel. It'll be cool." Said Ian.

"Freezing more like. Let's get fucking in. Spliff time."

"Amen to that, brother."

CHAPTER 10

TOMMY

Tommy looked at the small piece of paper he held uncertainly between the thumb and index finger of his right hand. About a quarter of the size of a postage stamp, it was a washed out purplish colour, with a butterfly barely visible in the centre. It looked like... nothing. Just a small scrap of paper. Insignificant. Yet the longer he looked, the more he felt his own butterflies build in his stomach. Innocuous as it appeared, he had heard the stories of what this could do. Hallucinations, communing with God, demons, madness. He'd always viewed drugs as a sordid business. Junkies; contemptible, pathetic figures, too weak and self-indulgent to function in the real world where hard work and accepting responsibility were what made the world go round, a world junkies just wanted to escape, to annihilate. But this seemed different somehow. More scientific. More of an exploration. An adventure.

After some consideration and coercion from his fellow explorers, it was decided there was nothing else to do. He quickly popped the tab into his mouth and washed it down with a sharp gulp of wine. Then he waited. And waited. Nothing. Ten minutes passed, twenty, thirty, do you feel anything yet? No, do you? No. Thirty minutes, nothing yet, I think they're duds, we've be conned......then, after about an hour, when all seemed lost, it happened. First he became aware of a warm...ache spreading through his body, not unpleasant, almost gnawing him as he clenched his teeth, his mouth dry. The lights and TV became brighter and brighter, sharper and more detailed. And more...interesting. He looked deeper at the people on the TV screen till they dissolved into patterns of shapes and colours, each shimmering with an existence of its own, its own space, its own life, till it died making way for the next one just like life, just like all of us going round and round this wheel of craziness, pointlessness, what is the point, but there must be because people are such amazing things, have done such amazing things, listen to that music, fucking awesome, genius, how can you hear that, really hear it and not believe in God? The sound going round and round, aural love in every sailing, swerving, caressing, beautiful note and Hendrix is a god spreading love in his own way, the only way he can, but do people care? All you hear is murder, rape, brutality, where's the love? The intensity expanded throughout his senses. His body awash with pleasure, thoughts racing faster and faster, yeeess, just so fucking beautiful, it all made sense, humanity made sense, we were all one, the good, the bad, the ugly, even Hitler, devoid of even the most primal compassion, but like a fucking rock star in his own way, Nuremberg, working those frenzied adoring crowds like Freddie mercury, but to kill him, an assassin, sparing millions, innocent millions, murder as the ultimate act of love and peace, the ultimate hippie ideal, action, assassination, can murder be compassion? Can there be peace in life ebbing away from dulling, greying eyes, bye byes, no more mister blue skies, Oh fuck, yes!

As Tommy's mind raced, his attention turned to his friends as they laughed and joked together across the room, so far away, separate. He suddenly felt isolated, alone, as if in a different reality from the others. The laughter grew, as they looked over at him, faces twisted, grotesque. He smiled back, to join in, be part of it, join in the laughter, but it was artificial, he wasn't like them, they didn't understand, or know how he was feeling, thinking, how could they, he was alone, we're all alone and they couldn't help him, no one could. Why couldn't he feel like they felt? What was the matter with him? The joy, empathy, lightness, spontaneity. So natural, but not to him, not to the alien. He tried to calm down, breathing slowly, still smiling so no one would know; no one would cause a fuss. The more he tried to act and think normally, the more abnormal he felt, and with this the seeds of anxiety were sown, growing into fierce, unstoppable panic. Sweat began oozing from his every pore as he wrestled with his mind, desperately trying to keep it together and keep it to himself. Telling the others would only amplify it; he had to contain it, the fear, the dread. What had he done? He looked at his watch. Only two hours had passed since that simple act of bravado. Hadn't Stevie said it lasts for ten, sometimes even a whole day? How could he endure for such an eternity when every second had suddenly become a struggle for survival? He got up and went to the toilet, trying not to give the game away, but the more he tried, the more exposed he felt. He closed the door, unzipped his fly and watched the stream of urine escape, abandoning his body as he himself yearned to do. He looked again at his watch and felt his anxiety raise further with the realisation that only a further five minutes had passed. Another loud roar of laughter erupted, generating another wave of fear to carry him further from safety. He knew that he had to at least eliminate the struggle of trying to act normal. If he could be alone he could relax. He had to leave. He picked up his coat and quietly opened the door, only partially closing it behind him, afraid any noise would bring discovery, questions, and further alienation.

The street was deserted in peaceful slumber, however he soon realised that only his friends had been left behind. Now with no distractions, anxiety, his unwelcome companion commanded his undivided attention, a hitcher, unhinged, threatening, out of control, refusing to leave. He stopped for a second but knew he couldn't go back, so he started running, slowly at first, then faster and faster as he tried in vain to escape his tormentor, through the moon-lit streets of fear. Soon he was standing outside his front door. Hesitating for a minute, he inserted the latchkey, opening the door slowly, closing it behind him as quietly as he could. He paused. He looked at himself in the hall mirror, closer, his eyes huge black pools. What have I done to you? He turned and opened the living room door, trying to appear normal. "I'm just going to bed. I've got a sore head." There was no one there. Having other things on his mind he hadn't noticed their car wasn't in the driveway. Guess they were having a good time at Auntie Cathy's. Relief was quickly overtaken by the fear of their imminent arrival. He had to get to his room and Sanctuary. He ran up the stairs shutting the door firmly behind him. He switched the light on and looked around, but all familiarity had been replaced by an other-worldliness, the room's interior stolen and a forgery substituted in its place. Everything was where it should be, had the correct shape, but there the similarity ended. Previously inanimate objects shone with an almost living energy, glowing and flickering…watching. Every blink was a blinding flashgun. He switched the light off before his parents returned and came up for a chat. Pretend to be asleep. Sleep, how he prayed for sleep, begged for sleep. He closed his eyes, but what he had seen remained just as vivid even in darkness. Even in his mind there was no escape, no peace. The realisation that he had lost control of even that basic security barrier pushed him deeper into overwhelming panic and despair. He looked his watch. Peering through the dimness, his heart sank. 10 o'clock. He knew he still had hours to go, but it would feel like years. He suddenly understood hell. It wasn't some pit in the depths of the earth. It was here and now in the depths of the human mind. Suddenly suicide emerged from the shadows offering relief from a wretched eternity of torment. Acceptance seemed inevitable such was his wretchedness. Its certainty chilled him and he desperately tried to think of another way out. If he couldn't sleep, he had to find another path to unconsciousness, to oblivion. He clenched his right hand firmly to form a fist, pulled it back and slammed it against his chin. He repeated it a further three times, to no avail. His mind reminded him of the bottle of paracetamol downstairs in the kitchen drawer. He sat upright and tried to get a grip, to control his thoughts as they had been controlling him, consciously, forcefully, he turned his mind to happier times, summer trips with his parents, the beach, fish and chips, ice cream, hanging out with Stevie, the fun they had had. Gradually he found he could vividly recapture the images almost like stepping back in time. He could also manipulate them, as living dreams under his control. Gradually the frantic trip slowed, fear gently dissipating, losing its power, loosening its grip, allowing the transfer of control back once more to Tommy, bringing safety, peace and priceless relief.

As time passed, he felt a deep sense of contentment and warmth fill him. With the effects of the drug reduced, he began to enjoy it once more, manipulating and controlling its effects. Casting aside grandiose spiritual or scientific concerns, he turned his attention to Sharon and to the night they were alone together. This time in his mind, in full 3D empathic acid vision, everything was perfect. Then, both satisfied, they smiled, kissed and fell asleep.

But his hard won peace would be short lived.

CHAPTER 11

The streets were still silent except for some early bird-song as Stevie made his way home, deserted but for an old man in a thrown together house coat and slippers, straining to hold onto the chocolate brown Labrador desperately trying to escape, or at least have some privacy to take a dump. Stevie grinned to himself, wondering what it would be like to have someone watch you squatting on someone's lawn, firing one out. If dogs had a sense of shame they hid it damn well. A dog's life. Sleep, eat, more sleep, walk, shit, piss, escape, sniff, hump, more sleep. Didn't sound too bad. As he walked on he suddenly felt the acid coming back up in the fresh air. A major brain rush. God he felt good. He felt God. Everything was perfect. No fear, no confusion, no alienation. Perfect connection. Perfect clarity. Suddenly he began to run, slowly at first, then faster and faster. He felt like he could fly. He jumped high into the air, travelling what seemed like miles, before returning gently to earth. He wished he could fly forever, escaping earth's gravity never to return. Behind him the old man and the dog, now sitting obediently, pressed pause and watched the boy doing the long jump at one o'clock in the morning. With a baffled shake of the head they turned their backs and returned to the serious business of public fouling. Plastic bags? I don't think so. When it came to dog crap, Mr Morrison was strictly old school.

Reaching the end of the road, the footbridge before him stood rigid and tense as if expecting him, and he was late. He leapt up the stairs 2, 3 at a time and ran across, turning to look at the road beneath before stopping sharply. Drawn to the side of the bridge he walked slowly to the edge, held the handrail and watched. The road was quiet, traffic infrequent. He stood serenely as the headlights edged over the horizon, closing in, hurtling towards him before disappearing with a desperate scream beneath him leaving only echos dissolving in the night air. He watched and watched as his people, roaring lost souls, raced from one futile gesture to the next. So sad, so tragic, so needless. He knew he could help them. No one else could. Only he had clear sight of this world, filled with tricks and delusions. He had to help them, to stop them, to explain what was going on, going wrong with life, their lives. He had to stop them. He ran back down the steps and climbed frantically over the wire mesh fence, stopping to look up the road, feeling himself filled with love. He felt it rush through him, building in the pit of his stomach, his divine benevolence radiating out in all directions. Stevie smiled, sighed...and walked out onto the road. Stopping in the centre of the oncoming carriageway, he turned to face the oncoming congregation as they approached one at a time. On this spot he would build the foundations of his church. He waved his hands, beckoning his people to join him. However, approaching at speed, the drunken James Paterson's attention quickly focused on evasion as he jerked the wheel violently to the right narrowly missing his saviour. He breathed deeply, calming his racing heart, thanking God for his lucky escape, but God had other plans and his eyes widened in horror as Jean and Danny Slater's Ford Fiesta suddenly appeared from a blind bend towards him. Disbelief filled them as Danny braked hard, jerking the wheel to miss the mad man driving towards him, but lady luck had gone home early, leaving them to their crunching metal, screams and silence. Even the birds fell silent, as if unsure what to say at a time like this.

For James the world stopped in shocked disbelief. He sat not knowing anything, shut down before shock was replaced by panic. What had he done? He decided to find out...but soon wished he hadn't. The scene was a Damien Hirst sculpture in metal and meat. But there were no admirers here commenting on composition and pushing of boundaries. He stared in horror, firstly at the bleeding woman, obviously dead, then away from the car at the body on the ground. Was he alive? Then he saw the head and screamed. "Oh my God, Oh my god, oh my God," he repeated over and over. He paced back and forth trying to get a grip, thoughts spiralling out of control. "Fuck, fuck, fuck. I need to get out of here. If I get breathalysed. They're dead, I can't do anything. Fuck!" He turned to his car, checking the damage, sighing with relief. He had decided to buy a Lexus because of their good safety record and wept at his good judgement. The car, although bashed front right, had emerged in much better shape than the Slater's mangled wreck. It might even be driveable he whispered in his mind, barely daring to hope. He turned the key back, then hesitating for a moment, he turned it forward and the engine purred to life, lurched forward, and then stalled. "Fuck!" Putting it in neutral, he re started the engine, pressed the clutch, put it in gear and moaned with relief as the car moved forward. But then he stopped. There were two dead people, he should call someone, he couldn't just leave. But if he did he'd go to jail, lose his job, wife, everything. They were dead, so what was the point. It wasn't even his fault, but they wouldn't see it that way. It wasn't his fault. Suddenly his mind returned to the nutter standing in the middle of the road. "Where is that cunt, this is his fucking fault!" He looked over to see Stevie still standing in the middle of the road, arms now by his side, motionless, watching. Their eyes met for a second time. Stevie began to walk slowly towards him. James turned to get out of the car, rage filling him but quickly dissipating as car headlights appeared in the distance. He had to get out of there and quickly. He shoved the car into gear and sped off, cursing as he realised he was still on the wrong side of the road. But what about the car? How would he explain it to his wife? The police would be looking for a bashed car. But he couldn't think straight. "Let's get it in the garage tonight. Tomorrow...fuck." he muttered as no answer came.

As Stevie approached, he gazed solemnly at the scene before him. It was as if a child had scattered their toys in a fit of frustrated fury, pulling the head off one for good measure. But he knew these were no toys, and he watched the blood leave the broken bodies, life draining with it. Human beings were so delicate, life so fragile. It was a miracle we lasted so long, crash test dummies ignorant of the violence surrounding us. He knelt down and dipped his finger in the blood, studying it closely, tasting it. Life. Suddenly his attention was drawn to an object a few yards away where the other car had been. He walked over bent down and picked it up. A small piece of card. He squinted in the dim light and then smiled. His disciple, James Paterson, branch manager. But he too knew he had to leave, as the accusing glare of the approaching car closed in. He put it in his pocket and disappeared into the bushes.

Then he flew home.

CHAPTER 12

Stevie slowed down as he approached his destination, pausing for a moment to absorb the row of small, uniform council houses that had been the cradle of his entire life. He felt a mix of fuzzy, warm nostalgia and gentle pity for the inhabitants, bound to this place by ignorance and fear of the outside world, unknown terrors lurking amongst the endless opportunities. He gently turned the handle, opened the door and walked inside. In front of him a grey-haired dwarf was hopping on one leg trying desperately to get the other into his trousers, but ending up on the threadbare carpet. A moment later, Margo McDaid opened the bedroom door, holding onto the frame for support. She swayed slowly, trying to focus on the events unfolding in the gloom. Giving up, she reached out and switched on the light, recoiling sharply at the sudden glare. Stevie did likewise at the sight of his mother in a shocking pink baby doll nightie, apparently naked from the waist down, the ravages of time and self-abuse on full display. Even the realisation that her sagging stomach was in fact obscuring a matching pink G string did little to pretty the picture. Breathing in deeply, Margo finally spoke. "Get tae bed you."

Unable to get the second leg in, the leprechaun lothario began crawling towards his giant mistress.

"Not you, action man!"

The man stopped dead.

"You shagged a dwarf...." mumbled Stevie, in foggy transition between two worlds.

A slap across the face and the transition was complete.

"He's not a dwarf, he's just a wee man. He's taller standing up."

"Eh? Everybody's taller standing up."

"I am standing up," offered the wee man, now vertical.

"Fuck off home tiny. I thought you people were supposed to be like tripods. I never felt a thing."

"No wonder, I nearly fell in." Instantly filled with regret he turned to run, but instead fell foul of his re-descending trousers. His buttocks oscillated furiously as his carpet burning knees desperately tried to carry him to freedom. Then, just as escape seemed a possibility, Margo jumped forward and kicked him hard between the legs, slamming the door behind him as he rolled head over heels into the street.

"He probably buys his clothes in Mother-care," laughed Stevie.

Another slap removed the desire for further observation.

"Where have you been til this time, it's...what time is it?"

"I was just down at Ian's."

"Ian! What have I said about hanging about....Wait a minute. Wait a fucking minute!" She grabbed hold of his head, twisting it, turning his face towards her. Studying, focusing as intently as her inebriated state would allow. "Ya

71

wee bastard you. Look at your eyes. They're like fucking saucers. Flying fucking saucers!" she yelled, her pun passing her by. "You've taken something. Drugs! That's what it is. You're on fucking drugs! I don't believe this. What have you took? You should know better. Have you ever seen me taking drugs?"

Stevie ...thought better of it.

"You're getting your stomach pumped!" Stevie stared in horror. "No way. No way, I'm fine, I haven't taken anything, Mam I promise, I'm fine, I'm fine, honest."

"You're a liar! You could have took poison for all you know!"

"Honest, Mam, I haven't. I swear to God!"

Margo paused for a second. She was in no fit state to drive and the sight of an ambulance at the door; she'd be the talk of the street for weeks. She thought as hard as her drink-addled brain would allow, before a solution popped up.

"Don't move," she commanded, walking to the kitchen. A few moments later she returned clutching a pint glass containing a cloudy liquid.

"Drink this. All of it."

"What is it?"

"Just fucking drink it."

"Not till you tell me what it is"

"Salt water, it'll make you sick, now drink it!"

"No way." Stevie suddenly found himself transported into the Russian roulette scene from the Deer hunter.

"Drink!" she barked, slapping him. "Drink!" slap, "Drink!" slap, "Drink!", slap.

Then just like in the movie, he caved. "Okay! Okay!" He paused for a moment, then, just before the next slap, he drank, and drank, and drank, till the glass was empty. They both stared at each other for a moment, Stevie fighting to hold it down, to show his defiance. Then, at the first hint of triumph on Stevie's face, Margo played the ace.

"I also pissed in it."

A second later Margo stood like an entrant in the wet t-shirt contest of nightmares. "You've ruined it," she wailed, surveying the soaked nightie.

"You pissed in it?!"

"I just made that up."

As a smile made another tentative entrance, it was slapped on its way.

"Stop slapping me, for fuck sake."

"Where did you get it?"

"I told you, I haven't taken anything."

Slap. "It was Ian wasn't it," Slap, "wasn't it!? I'm going tae break his fucking legs. You get to your fucking bed. Now!"

All fight knocked out of him, he turned meekly and walked, condemned to his cell.

Margo however was only just getting warmed up.

CHAPTER 13

With all concerns over drink-driving tossed into
the bin of inconvenience, Margo McDaid's car
screeched to a halt outside the front door of 15
Park Street, before she sprang out and
proceeded to give it a pounding not seen since
the days of vintage Tyson. After 23 seconds of
the first round, the door, battered and broken,
gave up all resistance and crashed to the floor.
Bursting in and with an almost religious zeal, she
kicked open every room door in turn, looking for
signs of life.

Weasel McPhee was crouched behind the
kitchen table. He'd turned up at Ian's an hour
earlier looking for a place to crash, declining his
friends drug induced proposal of a night under
canvas in favour of his far comfier couch. Bad
timing. Bad choice. Weasel was a wiry 25 year
old, who'd long lost any semblance of youth. His
arms and face, heavily marked and scabbed,
looked as tatty and worn out as the clothes that
covered his emaciated frame. In short, his
appearance screamed junkie. Not a good look for
his current predicament. Wincing repeatedly, he
battled to maintain control of his bodily
functions, a battle he was losing with every
passing door. Margo McDaid exploded into the
small but impressively stained kitchen like
Cruella DeVille on meth, her heavy breath the
only sound in a short moment of silence as she
scanned every visible inch of the room. Then she

noticed the egg boiling in the pot and her eyes widened.

"Where the fuck are you?" she spat, turning to continue her search.

On hearing the sound of a woman's voice Weasel leapt to his feet with newfound bravado.

"What the fuck do you think you're doing you stupid bitch? Do you know where you are? Do you know who I am? "

In a life filled with mistakes this was merely the latest and Weasel's scream reached a dog-deafening pitch as the contents of the pot seared his genitals. Margo McDaid visibly calmed as she sat and watched the spectacle before her, Weasel ripping at his trousers, desperately dragging them down to his knees, the battle for bowel and bladder control all too visibly lost. He struggled to his feet, all the while gazing in disbelief at his rapidly blistering, lobster pink groin and its agony.

"Ahhhh, fuck, fuck , ahhhhhhhhh. What the fuck!?" wailed Weasel.

"Where's Ian?" snarled Margo.

Weasel ignored her request for information and struggled towards the cold tap. Margo's fury arose once more and the pot fell with equal intensity onto Weasels head breaking the pot from the handle and forcing Weasel to his knees.

"Fuck! What!? What!?"

"Where the fuck is Ian, dick head?!"

"I don't fucking know do I."

Margo began opening drawers until she found what she was looking for. Weasel's breath abruptly stopped as the blade made contact with the base of his already tender penis.

"Oh fuck, oh fuck, oh fuck…." muttered Weasel dementedly.

"Oh fuck indeed, "replied Margo with the calmness of the end game and certain victory.

"Camping! Camping! Up Blackstone hill."

"Camping? Has he joined the fucking boy scouts now?" sneered Margo with disbelief.

"No, I swear. Just himself, honest. Please just go. Leave me."

"Well he better have his tent pegs hammered in tight because hurricane Margo's coming his way!" Margo lowered the knife and turned to leave. As she did, Weasel leapt up to the sink, struggling to manipulate his groin under the running cold water and tantalising relief. Margo allowed herself the briefest of smiles before marching out the way she had come. Business was unfinished.

Margo felt her heart beat faster as Blackstone hill came into view. More of a small mound than a hill and containing no black stone whatsoever; it was however very popular as a place for illicit activities amongst the young and those who simply refused to grow up. Obscured by dense woodlands, underage drinking, drugging and a wide range of sexual activity where usually going on in some dark corner out of sight of anxious, paranoid suburbia and consequently the police, who rarely visited. It was also a place just to hide, to escape…and sometimes to camp.

Twisting the wheel of her VW Golf hard left, she struggled to focus as she hurtled through the long grass towards the trees, before braking sharply, skidding and coming to a stop inches from disaster. Yanking up the hand brake, Margo shoved open the door, staggered out and fell face first into the mud. Her pink leisure suit would need some intensive laundering but that could wait. Holding onto the car for support, she managed to slide her way to the boot from which she extracted a gleaming aluminium baseball bat. She smiled at it tenderly, stroking it gently along its length.

"If only that wee man had something like you eh," she whispered affectionately. "Let's take care of business first."

She ran towards the trees, immediately finding herself once more face down in the mud. "Bastard" she screamed. "Shit. Sssshh Margo, don't let the little runt hear you. Outsmart him. You're too fucking clever for that prick. Ssshh. For fuck sake, Margo, shut up. Ok, ok," she muttered to herself.

Plunging into the trees and undergrowth she bullied her way through, cursing, hacking, grabbing as she went, then chastising herself for her lack of stealth, only to immediately forget and repeat the cycle. Any living thing that could run did, the rest, literally rooted to the spot, awaited their assault. Fifteen minutes later she finally emerged from the other side, muddied, scratched and mad as hell. She stopped and surveyed the wreckage of her beloved pink attire, cursing herself for wearing it, and Stevie for…..fucking everything. She reached into her pocket and pulled out a quarter bottle of supermarket own brand vodka, took three gulps then looked around for her prey, but saw only grass. It crossed her mind that weasel had lied, but she saw the terror in his eyes, he wasn't going to put his dick on the line to protect someone else. It wasn't in his nature. She inhaled deeply and, knowing the only way was up, started climbing. She scanned the terrain as she went, looking up, across, down, making herself dizzy in the process, occasionally stumbling to her knees, cursing. Then as she neared the summit the first sight of the canvas peak appeared. She immediately fell to her knees and began crawling commando style towards the tent. "What the fuck are you doing Margo? Get a grip, it's not a fucking hostage rescue, silly old cow. "She clambered to her feet, paused for a second to regain her balance and then, standing as upright as she could, swaggered slowly and deliberately towards her unsuspecting victim, baseball bat slung over her shoulder until finally she was in range. Taking another deep breath she swung hard through the canvas, till the bat thudded against the ground. Again she swung, then again and again. Thud after thud, but no screams, no yells of pain. She stopped and went to the tents entrance and quickly pulled down the zip. Empty. But there was a tent. And where there was a tent there was a camper. But where? She turned all round. Nothing. But she hadn't come all this way for nothing. He was here and she would find him. She set off over the hill top and there he was, standing 20 feet away, stripped to his underwear, head tilted towards the stars, his back to the slowly approaching Margo now in full stealth mode. As he was giving himself a quick post piss shake, he heard a noise behind him and turned. The startled pair suddenly found themselves face to face, momentarily bewildered before Margo broke the silence.

"Come here you!" she commanded, grabbing the back of his hair and pulling him towards her......before forcing her tongue deep into the startled young mouth. The baseball bat dropped to the ground as her hand latched roughly around his dangling member. She frenziedly jerked it, desperately trying to bring it to life, to be of service, but to no avail. Frustrated, lust was cast aside and fury re-instated. Reaching beside her she gripped the firm shaft of the weapon and swiftly whipped it into Ian's leg. His daze was shattered by the piercing jolt of pain, hopping in agony as Margo stumbled.

"What the..."

But this was no time for Q&A. He bolted with Margo close behind, swinging wildly. As he too stumbled, a ping rang out through the still night. Then she fell and escape seemed assured until another stumble, another ping, another scream, Margo trying to knock Ian's head for a home run.

Meanwhile on the other side of town, there would be another knock, another scream.

CHAPTER 14

As the door was knocked again, more and more adrenalin dumped into Tommy's bloodstream, turbo-charging a disintegrating nervous system, his mind in full-blown anarchy. He breathed deeply trying desperately to regain control, to win the battle he thought was over, trying to divert his mind away from how he felt to what was happening, to be logical. Nothing had happened. Who knows why the police were there, maybe the wrong door, maybe nothing serious. But the panic raging through his body was too strong for his mind to ignore, which left disguise as the only strategy. But even his little sister could see through that.

"You ok Tommy? Have you done something? Or Stevie?" she quizzed.

"No, nothing, nothing. Go on down and see what they want."

"Eh?" replied the startled little girl. "I eh…"

Tommy winced at his sisters stare, part accusing, part pleading. A jolt of self-loathing snapped his mind out of panic, into something nobler.

"Sorry sis, I don't know what I was thinking. Not quite woken up yet, eh?" His voice steadying with a hint of a forced smile. But a hint was enough and his sister's tension and questioning eased.

"You wait here. I'll go down and see what they want." He pensively walked out the door and down the stairs, not seeing his sister follow behind. Another round of bangs, growing louder as he approached.

"I'm coming! I'm coming!" he yelled. He took a deep breath and opened the door. In front of him were a man and a woman in normal, if formal, attire. Tommy felt momentarily confused until he noticed the two uniformed police men behind them standing beside their car. Momentary eye contact was quickly broken as both men lowered their gaze, studying the roads worn and damaged surface with practised intensity.

"Sorry to wake you up at this hour. May we come inside?" asked the woman gently.

"Eh. Yeah, okay," Tommy stuttered, trying to appear normal. He turned towards the living room and put the light on. "Would you like a cup of tea?" he asked, before chastising himself. What the hell was he thinking? Let's get them out quick, for fuck's sake. To his relief, both politely declined.

"Are you on your own?" asked the man.

"No, I'm here; I'm his sister," blurted Susie, coming into view.
The man and woman looked at each other, a pained weary expression appearing for a moment, before being consciously subdued.

"Eh, I think it would be better if we talked alone, maybe the little one would be better in bed," suggested the woman solemnly.

"I was in bed till you tried to knock the door down!" yelled Susie, frightened, sensing something terrible had happened.

"Susie! Go to bed!" shouted Tommy, startled by her outburst.

"But..."

"Now, Susie," quieter this time, sensing her fear.

"Maybe a relative could come over?" the man suggested, before realising his gaff.

"What do you mean? I'm here. What's this about? Are you taking me away?" More adrenaline pumped into Tommy's system.

"No, no, nothing like that," replied the woman, trying to regain control of the situation. Of the procedure.

"Anyway mum and dad will be back soon so...Why are you here?"

"I really think the little one would be better in bed," interrupted the woman.

"Sis."

"Ok, ok, I'm going."

The two officers paused for a moment. The man then went over to the door, gazed up the stairs, then, when satisfied, closed the door and sat down.

"I'm DS Brown and this is DC Macgregor."

"May I ask your name?"

"Tommy."

And your surname?"

"Slater. Tommy Slater."

And the mum and dad you mentioned, what were their names?" asked DC Macgregor.

DS Brown shot another piercing stare at her colleague, sighing in disbelief, quickly interjecting in a vain attempt at damage limitation, but too late.

"What are your parents' names Tommy?"

"What did he mean were.... what's this about?" Tommy felt his phantom fears disperse, forced aside by a sense of dread firmly rooted in this reality.

"If you could just tell us their names please?" asked DS Brown, almost pleading.

Tommy paused, believing for a moment that if he didn't tell them, then...but he knew he had to. "Danny and Jean," he whispered anxiously, voice trembling.

"Sorry, could you repeat that?" asked DC Macgregor.

"I heard him!" snapped DS Brown, losing patience.

Tommy stared at one then the other, waiting. Waiting for answers, confirmation his life was about to fall apart.

"I'm sorry Tommy," began DS Brown, "but I'm afraid your parents were involved in a car accident earlier this evening."

Tears filled his eyes unnoticed as he asked the question he already knew the answer to. "Are they....ok?"

"I'm sorry Tommy. I'm afraid they were both killed."

Tommy slumped in his chair.

"They didn't suffer son, they were both killed instantly."

Tommy nodded his head, numb. "What happened?"

"Looks like they collided with another vehicle, which then drove off. We'll get them though son, don't you worry," DC Macgregor replied.

Tommy sat unresponsive, gazing at the carpet, the darkness of it.

"Is there anyone who can look after you? A relative, friend, someone nearby, a neighbour, maybe?"

"I'm Seventeen," Tommy replied quietly.

"Even so Tommy, we'd like to get someone in to be with you, just for a little while. An older person."

Tommy remained silent for a moment, unable to rationalise, before mumbling. "Margo, next door."

CHAPTER 15

It was a worn and torn Margo that turned her car
into the home straight, to be suddenly brought
into sharp focus by the flashing lights before her.
Unsure what to do, she did nothing, just kept on
going past the cars parked outside her home
until she felt safely out of range. She then parked
and adjusted her mirrors for maximum visibility.
There were two strange cars, one with flashing
lights, the other without, but connected. She
watched as four people, two in uniform, milled
about outside. Had she been seen? Reported by
some curtain twitcher, or some twat out walking
his dog? Suddenly the plain clothed pair
disappeared into a doorway. Jean Slater's
doorway. She smiled and watched as the
uniforms got back in their car, turned the
flashing lights off and drove away. The coast was
clear. She decided to leave her car where it was.
That way, if the cops made a sharp exit before
she reached safety, she could say she was out for
a walk....cross country....through mud, bushes
....falling several times in the process. No crime
in that. She opened the car door, closed it gently
behind her and power walked with all available
speed to her front door before pulling the key
out of her pocket. At the fourth attempt she got it
in the lock and turned it. She was in.
Suddenly all of the night's exploits caught up
with her as she was overwhelmed by exhaustion.
She barely managed to change into some old and

faithful PJ's and roll into bed before quickly losing consciousness. Soon she began to dream, music in the distance, getting closer....closer....so familiar...yes...she remembered...Beethoven's 5th...getting louder.

"Mrs McDaid!"

Confusion turned to comprehension as the doorbell rang again. (A gift from Bob Young.) "For fuck's sake, give me peace!" She looked at the clock. She'd been asleep for barely twenty minutes. "Who the fuck is that, at this time?"

"Mrs McDaid! It's the police, can we have a word?" came the answer.

Margo was now too exhausted to care. They could lock her up for a hundred years; fuck it, as long as she could get her head down. She staggered to the door and opened the latch. The eyes of the officers widened at the sight before them. Margo paused, turned to look in the hall mirror, before returning to the police officers. "Us girls and our beauty treatments eh," she offered by way of explanation of the thick layers of mud smeared across her face and hair. "And do they appreciate it?" she continued, nodding towards the male officer. "Do they f....Oh, don't mind me."

"Mrs McDaid. It is Mrs McDaid isn't it?" enquired DS Brown.

"Ms McDaid, but please call me Margo, for that is my name. Now what is it my awakening can assist you both with? Always happy to help the nation's finest, and that is what you are lady and gentleman," slurred Margo, hand resting on the hall table for support.

"Eh, may we come in Ms Mc...sorry, Margo."

"Certainly, certainly, me casa, su casa as we say in Italy."

"Are you from Italy?"

"No, Govan. Right this way. Excuse the untidiness of my humble abode. I've been having a wee spring clean. Better late than never eh?" The officers looked around in amazement at what looked like a laundrette, moments after hurricane Katrina had struck.

"Sorry we've interrupted you."

"Just chuck stuff out the way and make yourselves comfortable."

The bewildered pair searched for comfort underneath the bizarre and garish outfits. Just as DC Macgregor had managed to create a space amongst the chaos, his colleague spoke.

"Actually we won't take up any more of your time. All I really wanted to do was check whether Tommy next door is seventeen."

"Tommy?...Eh...yes, that's right, the same age as my Stevie."

Just at that, her Stevie entered.

"What's going on Mam?" He asked, squinting, eyes adjusting to the light.

DS Brown sighed and cleared some space to sit. It was going to be a long night. "I'm afraid I have some bad news."

CHAPTER 16

The next morning, Stevie awoke, unsure if he had even been asleep. The thick fog still hanging over his mind rendered his thinking opaque. He struggled to focus. He sat upright in the chair where he'd spent the latter half of the night, the comfort of his bed seeming an inappropriate luxury. He looked over to the settee where his mother lay, partly sleeping, but mainly just unconscious. He examined her, studying the lines etched deep into her face by years of indulgence, her hair dyed yet another colour never seen in nature. He stared intently at a thin stream of drool trickling from the corner of her mouth, down her chin to the expanding damp patch on her cushion. Beyond that was...shapeless, pink and velour. A fitting epitaph. But there was love beneath the superficial contempt. It was easy to dismiss her as trash, with all her vulgarity and excesses, but he knew that she had raised him alone and would die for him, or if necessary kill for him. The hint of a smile bloomed for a warm fuzzy moment but soon withered as the significance of his mother sleeping there dispersed the fog, sleeping there, not in her bed, not in the bed occupied by Tommy and Susie Q, desperately hanging on to each other for dear life, painfully awake with eyes tight shut.
The enormity of what had happened finally began to light up his brain. "Fuck no," he whispered to no one. His mind sparked like a

pinball machine. How the fuck did this happen? What's going to happen to them? Where are they going to live? It was all fucked. They must be... What's going on in their heads? Fidgeting in the chair, his agitation grew as he rocked back and forth; holding his head, going over the previous night's events as best he could, rage eliminating all other emotional rivals who would dare muddy the moral waters. I mean, one minute you're just having a laugh with your mates, just another day, then some fucking arsehole in a car just loses it, kills two innocent people, and then legs it! I couldn't say anything. The cops might try to get funny, pin it on me. No way. Talking wouldn't do any good anyway. Even if they found the guy, it would be one word against the other, it's not going to bring them back is it, so why risk it. Why fuck up my life. It wasn't my fault. Life goes on, that's all there is to it. The guy must have been pissed. Must have been, driving like a maniac. "Fucking cunt!" he snarled.

"You say something, Son?" Margo tilted her head towards him, taking in all she could through one half opened eye, hoping such a small gesture of consciousness would go unnoticed and she could fall once more into oblivion.

"No Ma, go back to sleep."

But she already had. He got up and wove around the assorted debris till he reached the bathroom. Bladder emptied, he studied the face in the mirror, staring deep into the black vacuous eyes of the stranger staring straight back, their message clear, "I don't know what you're looking for, Son, but you ain't gonna find it here." Then he noticed something in his hair. "Dragged through a hedge backwards, right enough," he muttered in a vain attempt at lifting his mood. He put his hand in his pocket and pulled out a black plastic comb to straighten things out. As he did, something else caught his eye. He watched as a small card fluttered to the floor. His eyes narrowed, squinting as he bent to pick it up. Then he remembered. His thumb and index finger gripped the card tightly, as if trying to crush the life from it. "You're fucking mine now…Mine."

On the way back to the living room Stevie paused at his mother's bedroom door. He quietly turned the handle and opened it just enough to see Tommy and Susie laying face to face on top of the covers, eyes still closed, knowing they were awake but easier all round just to play along. He had no idea what to say to them anyway. Besides, he was going to give them more than all the pointless platitudes and condolences that would be coming their way over the next week or two. He'd give them justice. But for now, Mr James Paterson, branch manager could wait.

CHAPTER 17

8 am. James Paterson stared through his bedroom ceiling into the empty darkness beyond, beads of cold sweat gathering on his forehead, trickling down to his sodden pillow. He had long given up trying to compose himself, each demand to just get a grip swept away in this synaptic Tsunami. Time crawled and sprinted all at the same time. He hadn't moved a muscle since locking the evidence in the garage and slipping silently beneath the covers, beside his mercifully sleeping wife. But there had been no mercy since. He had forgone his usual pyjamas for fear of disturbing her, and now the whole bed beneath him was sodden with his fear and dread. He saw the faces of the helpless pair, their terror turning to accusation. But it wasn't his fault; it was that mad fucking psycho. Ok, he had been drinking, but it wouldn't have made any difference. It would still have been the same outcome. The same bloody, disfigured, world-destroying outcome. But people wouldn't see it like that. Even one point over the limit and all people would see would be a drunk driver involved in a fatal crash. No shades of grey. Guilty! But soon no one would know he'd been drunk. He'd be sober soon. But he'd left the scene. It was a hit and run. Ok there was nothing he could do, they were both obviously dead, but…."so why did you run? If it wasn't your fault, Sir?" A sarcastic "Sir", because they would know.

Why else would he have run? He tried again to pacify his mind. What's done is done. Damage limitation. They're dead, he's alive, but his life would be over if he couldn't figure out a way to erase the big fucking sign in the garage. The sign pointing straight at him screaming "Murderer this way", in twisted metallic letters. He had to get rid of it, but how? He was supposed to be going shopping with his wife that afternoon. Think James, think. His mind stepped up a gear, turbo-charged by blind adrenal panic. How was it possible to think so much, yet fail to form a single cohesive thought? I need to sleep, switch off. "Good luck with that killer", sniggered his mind. On and on and on and fucking on. He turned and looked at the clock. 10 am. Fuck. How can....then his wife turned in the bed. He stopped breathing. Don't wake up, please don't wake up. She woke up.

"What time did you get in?" she whispered sleepily.

"Eh...not late...must have been just after you got to bed."

She turned towards him. "Eagh, you're soaking wet!"

"Eh... yes...I think I'm coming down with something. I don't feel very well... I don't think I'll be able to go shopping today."

"Ooh James, you promised."

"I know, but you don't want me sweating over all the shirts and stuff do you?"

"No, but...I suppose," she sighed. Jane Paterson turned back over, damp and disappointed. Her

93

big day out washed out before it began. Another weekend of nothing opening up before her. "I'll just go myself, I really need to get some new clothes, and I'll get you some bits and pieces. If they don't fit I can take them back."

His heart sank. One hurdle jumped, another thrown in his path. Think dammit. "You can't," he spluttered."

"Why not?"

"Eh…it's the car….it's…eh… not running right. Kept cutting out. I was lucky to make it home."

"Well, what are you going to do? You'll need it for work on Monday?"

"Just leave it to me; I'll have a look at it."

"You? What do you know about cars?"

"I'll have a look anyway. Maybe it's something simple."

"It would need to be. I'll phone our Peter, get him to look at it."

"Just leave it, I'll look at it!" he barked.

"What's the matter with Peter looking at it, he's a mechanic, he won't mind. How many times has he said if we have any car problems don't go to a garage, he'd do it, no problem. You made him a fortune on those investments, which is more than you did, so I'm sure he'll be happy to repay the favour."

Fucking investments again. Speculate to accumulate is fine if you have something to speculate with. Not on his salary, with a wife, two kids and five credit cards to support. Think; think…"I'll take it up to him later," he replied, trying to buy some time.

"I thought it wasn't running?"

"I said it wasn't running right. I'll get it up there."

"I'm sure he won't mind coming down."

Another hurdle. Jump. "His tools and ramps are there. It would just be better."

"Ok, ok. Whatever."

How was he going to get it out without her seeing? Hurdle. Jump...."You can still go if you want."

"How can I go without a car? I'm not going by bus or train, carrying all those bags. They take too long, and I'd end up sitting next to some smelly old drunk."

"Take a taxi."

"A taxi? How much will that cost?"

"It doesn't matter; its fine, you haven't been out for a while, enjoy yourself."

A while, he thought to himself, a whole two weeks, but he had bigger problems than another hit to the wallet.

"You must be ill. Fine, I'll do that. What do you want me to get you?"

"Just...whatever you think."Because he couldn't.

After some silence they both got up to prepare for two very different days. Jane, patiently taking her time, selecting clothes, make up, each request for feedback met by a mumble or a grunt from James who sat tense and inert, waiting to put his plan into action as soon as she was gone, as soon as he'd thought of it.

The taxi's horn rang at 12 on the dot.

"Jane, that's the taxi."

"Ok, coming."

"You better hurry, he might go away."

"Don't be daft," she shouted from upstairs. "What's up with you today? Trying to get rid of me?"

"I just don't want you to....he's going!" He rushed to the door and ran out arms flailing. "Oi! stop! stop!"

The taxi drew up to the door. "Easy mate, I was just turning."

"Oh. Sorry, she's just coming."

"No worries mate."

As James walked back inside Jane descended in full make up, dressed in some of the purchases from her last retail therapy session. A fresh air kiss, some insincere pleasantries and she was gone. But now what? Now he had to find the answers, the big hurdle, the biggest of his life. How high could he jump?

After checking no one was passing, he went out to the garage, lifted the door...and it really was there, it had happened, it wasn't just a nightmare. The truth was there in every crease of buckled scraped metal, its disfigurement mirroring that of its victims. It wasn't his fault and it wasn't fair, but righteous indignation would have to wait. What was he going to do about it? He had to get it out of there. She would expect a fixed car when she got back and that wasn't going to happen. But what? Maybe he could take it somewhere and burn it. Say it was stolen. Maybe if he left it somewhere, someone would steal it. But why would he have left it? Did he really want to involve the police? Still more questions than answers. He had to get it out of here first. That much was certain. Break it down to small hurdles.

"Fuck it!"

He went back out, looked around. The coast was still clear. He got in the car, put on sunglasses and a baseball cap, started it up and reversed it out into the street. There was no time to shut the garage, he just turned and drove away, slowly, innocently. And he kept on diving, not knowing where he was going or what he was going to do when he got there. He slowed down to buy time, but a moment later was startled by a car horn, its driver yelling obscenities as he passed. Too slow James, don't attract attention. Think. Where to go? There was only one place to go. Where Jane expected him to go. If something happened anywhere else, it would raise suspicions. Another hurdle jumped. He turned the car and headed for Peter's. The final hurdle got higher and higher the closer he got to his brother-in-laws. He knew he couldn't go there for a very obvious reason.

"Eh, yes James, I think I've spotted the problem...."

His breathing became faster as his anxiety grew. Every street passed brought him closer to the end, every curious pedestrian a potential witness, their sideways glances fuelling panic and paranoia. All seemed hopeless, surrender inevitable with all its agonising consequences.

Then, suddenly, he found himself jolted out of autopilot. A dog hurtled out from a driveway up ahead barking, running hell for leather towards him with all its mongrel madness....and James knew what he had to do. Pressing hard on the accelerator he jerked the steering wheel sharp right turning the car directly into the path of the startled animal. Matched in madness, outmatched in brute force, the animal was propelled and crushed against a now partially demolished garden wall. After the noise of the impact subsided there came another eerie silence. After a few moments he heard a woman's voice, getting closer, becoming more and more hysterical.

"Mr Magoo...Mr Magoo...God...no!"

"He was well named! I swerved to try and avoid him but...Look what your bloody dog's done to my motor!"

CHAPTER 18

Tommy woke up many times the night before the funeral. When he awoke for the final time he got up with a fierce determination to do what he had to do. Thinking had run its course; it was now time to act. To take control. All thoughts of grief for his parents, of anxiety over what the future held for him and his sister were consciously and forcefully shut away. "Let's get this thing over with," he commanded himself.

He went to the bathroom, locked the door, peed, washed, and scrubbed his teeth with military vigour. He then combed his hair carefully before being distracted by his mirrored reflection. He looked pale, tired and drawn. He looked weak. Snapping out of it before self-pity descended, he straightened his shoulders and stood as tall as he could. Taking three deep breaths he continued attending to his hair, avoiding any further eye contact. No more slip-ups. He then returned to his room where he put on the clothes lying in a heap from the day before. The funeral uniform could wait.

Downstairs in the living room he looked at the clock. 9 O'clock. Fine. The funeral wasn't till 12.30. Car pick up at 12, assuming Margo hadn't cocked it up. Even if she had, he wasn't going to give her a hard time. For all her craziness she had been the ideal neighbour throughout this whole ordeal. Popping in from next door to keep an eye on them, she had always been there with a kind, supportive word, or a hug at the right time. Never overpowering, which surprised the hell out of him. She was there when needed, absent when she wasn't. As if that wasn't enough, she had also organised the whole funeral. But it also dawned on him that since the accident he'd never seen her having a drink, under the influence, or even noticed a hint of alcohol on her breath. For someone whose perfume was normally 70 proof, this was certainly out of the ordinary. Shock at the events? A short term sacrifice till after the formalities were over? Tommy neither knew nor cared. He only knew he would never forget.

Stevie, on the other hand, he'd barely seen. He'd never set foot in Tommy's house since the accident. When Tommy would go next door, Stevie had seemed distant and awkward, barely saying a word, unable to even look him in the eye. But what do you say to someone whose parents had just been wiped out in a car crash? A hit and run at that. What would he say? How would he react? Would he be any better? He reflected for a while, but no amount of excusing could completely eliminate his sense of being.... let down.

He went into the kitchen and put the kettle on. The great British ritual. The conviction that no problem, however overwhelming, could not be brought to its knees by a cup of tea. If nothing else, it was a simple act of normality and that would do for now. As he sat sipping, he looked around the room sighing as each piece of furniture, every picture and ornament became a silent storyteller, reviving memories of Saturday night's watching TV with his parents, playing with his toys, visits from gran, Hogmanay parties. He walked over to the cocktail cabinet in the corner, a remnant of the seventies. Opening it he took out a whiskey glass favoured by his Dad as he sang his party piece at New Year, sometimes with visitors, more lately without. He raised his eyes heavenward, putting the glass to his lips in silent toast. He then drifted pensively back to the present and to his sister. Barely sleeping and gripped by panic attacks when left on her own, he had, out of desperation, taken her to the doctors who prescribed some pills. These at least reduced her symptoms to an almost bearable level. He'd been reluctant to go down that route, but how much suffering was she supposed to bear, and yet putting his sister, a child, on tranquillisers? There was guilt there too as he knew there was an element of selfishness in his decision, the sight and sound of her pain more than he could stand. But there was no other choice to be made, he told himself. It was just til she was back to normal. Even with the pills, last night was the first night he'd managed to sleep in his own bed, albeit not the whole night, finally sneaking out of her room at 4am. He looked again at the clock. Ten. He drained his cup, put it back down on the brown plastic coaster and headed upstairs.

Susie lay as he had left her. On her right side, knees raised foetus like, clutching her favourite teddy tight to her chest. He thought about what to say to her when he woke her. What her mood would be like. He looked over to the bedside table and the bottle labelled diazepam. Valium and cornflakes, the perfect start to the day. Maybe today she'll feel better with a little bit of closure. He really didn't want her to be a zombie. Not today. Today was a day to say goodbye to mum and dad for the last time and with a clear head. He felt sure she would want that to. As he watched her sleep he smiled. It was the most peaceful he'd seen her since that night. But suddenly...

"They're dead, they're really dead!!" screamed Susie, suddenly sitting bolt upright as if possessed, eyes wide in terror. "I saw them Tommy! Tommy! I saw them!"

"It's ok, it's ok, I'm here, you were dreaming, it's just a nightmare, but it's ok, I'm here." Tommy pulled her close to him, but she pulled closer still, rocking back and forth. He steeled himself against the wave of anguish that threatened to drown him. Clenching his teeth, he faced it down. Normality wouldn't be returning any time soon.

Twelve o'clock came soon enough and Margo hadn't fucked up. The black Mercedes drew up outside their front door where the driver waited with practised solemnity. Tommy watched him from the window, waiting to see if he looked over, or looked at his watch, but no, this guy was no cabbie; he was a pro, the real deal. Transport and mourner in a single package. Tommy took his sisters hand, squeezed it gently and then guided his sedated sister out to face the toughest day of her young life. She held on tight, head lowered, eyes closed for the most part as she edged her way out. As Tommy opened the front door the driver opened his and walked round, opening the passenger door in readiness. Tommy was split between being impressed by his professionalism and contempt at the phoniness of it. Out of the corner of his eye he saw Margo and Stevie walking towards them, almost slow marching. He reigned in his cynicism, as it strained to unleash its bitter fury.

Once they were all secured in the back of the car, the driver pulled off on the slow drive to the crematorium. No one said very much. Tommy glanced up at Margo and Stevie, who smiled a sympathetic smile which he returned. Tommy had never seen Margo wear black before, but here she was, in a black trouser suit, power dressed to the max as if popping out for a funeral between board meetings. Stevie too was suited and booted, fidgeting, unused to such constriction. He'd never worn a tie before, not even to school, which after half a dozen warnings had finally given up.

"You two ok?" asked Margo, the pain visible in her eyes. No was plainly the answer but...

"Yes, fine."

Nothing else was said as the car slipped through the traffic on its short, dignified passage. As they reached the crematorium Tommy looked around the car park, his heart sinking as he surveyed the few cars dotted around. The driver repeated his earlier operation with similar precision and they exited with a thankful nod, Susie clinging to her brother, burying her face in his side, trying to hide from the world. As more men in black opened the doors, they walked down the aisle to take their seats at the front. Tommy looked around and began counting. A few familiar faces and a bald middle aged man he didn't recognise sitting at the back (why bother coming if you're going to sit back there, mister?). A grand total of twelve. He was filled with a mixture of anger and embarrassment. Not much to show for a life. Two lives. His mum and dad deserved better than this. Twelve fucking people. Ok, his parents were quiet, kept themselves to themselves, but they were good, kind, decent people. Where were Aunt Annie and Uncle Bill and his cousins, and most of their neighbours? He felt rage build up in him once more. It seemed the only way to get a good turnout at these things was to be an old soldier, join a church or play golf. Then you were guaranteed a showing. They turned out in their droves that lot, paying tribute to comrades fallen in the battle against Hitler, Satan or a bad handicap.

As the next professional guided him sombrely to his seat, his awareness returned to the reality of the day and the two coffins resting humbly before him. Two lives, a total of ninety three years of memories, hopes, dreams, happiness, sorrow and a lot of love, all came down in the end to two wooden boxes, a few bunches of flowers, a guy in a suit paid to look miserable, twelve people who looked miserable for free and some old git in a collar who was going to tell them all about people he had never met. He felt like screaming, storming out of the whole fucking phoney charade and never looking back. But go where? Where would be more real, honest, sincere...fair. And what of Susie? And his parents? They'd expect him to behave with dignity and decency as they had tried to live their own short lives. That is what the day demanded. So he sat back with his twelve comrades and let it go.

Except unknown to Tommy, there were now only eleven. Sitting alone in the back row, the stranger's heart had stopped as Stevie entered behind his friend. Disbelief quickly became panic as he waited for the sideways glance that would spell the end of him. He sat frozen, only his eyes moving, following their subject, willing him to keep looking forward, forward, a bit more, nearly there. When finally they took their seats, he slid silently with almost comic covertness along the pew before making his escape. Once outside he took a deep breath. What the hell had he been thinking, coming here? He didn't even know them.

But he had killed them.

CHAPTER 19

Stevie lay on his bed. Now that the funeral was out of the way his state of limbo had finally been lifted. The last few days had been a nightmare for him, trapped between the words he couldn't bring himself to say and the deeds he wanted to carry out. Every time he'd seen his friend or even thought of him, verbal impotence had overwhelmed him. What do you say to someone who'd experienced such devastating loss? Somehow "sorry mate" didn't seem to cut it. So rather than suffer such mutual awkwardness he'd just avoided the whole situation, but not the guilt that took its place. Not because it was his fault, because it wasn't, but he should be doing something to help his mate. And he would, he told himself, just not in a bunch of flowers kind of way. Actions speak louder than works was a cliché but also true. He stared at the business card in his hand, rubbing it between his thumb and forefinger. It was now time for action.

With Margo next door checking on her adopted brood, the house was empty. Stevie almost swaggered into the living room, sat down and picked up the phone. He took a deep breath, smiled and dialled. A lady's voice answered.

"Royal Bank of Scotland, Veronica speaking, how can I help?"

"Good morning Veronica, how are we today?"

"I'm fine thanks, and you?"

"Excellent."

"How can I help you today?"

"I'd like to make an appointment with Mr Paterson please."

"Can I ask what it is regarding?"

"A loan."

"One of our finance assistants will be able to help you with that."

Stevie paused. He hadn't considered that possibility. He thought for a moment.

"Actually it's for a rather large business loan and I'd really like to discuss it with Mr Paterson, if I may."

"Can you hold for a moment, please?"

"Certainly."

Stevie's heart began to race. He had thought it would be more straightforward than this. What would he do if the answer was no? Wait outside the bank and approach him? He could follow him home; look up his number in the book. Or maybe...

"Sorry to keep you sir. Can I ask your name please?"

"Eh..." Shit he hadn't thought of that. Don't give your real name for fuck sake. "Smith.... Sebastian Smith." Sebastian! Where the fuck had that come from?

"Mr Paterson can see you tomorrow at 10.30 if that's OK for you?"

"Yes, perfect. Tomorrow at 10.30 it is."

"See you tomorrow, Mr Smith."

"Please, call me Sebastian."

He sniggered to himself as he put the phone down.

The next morning, Stevie got up and left for school as normal, which at the moment meant alone as Tommy remained on compassionate leave. He'd been relieved to find it wasn't raining, in fact it was a beautiful day, the sky cloudless with a light breeze which would make the rising temperature comfortable as the day wore on. Instead of his usual journey, Stevie headed for the local park which, as it wasn't on any route to school, he hoped would be empty. As he approached, Lady Luck seemed to be smiling. There was one old man sitting alone on a bench, facing the opposite direction and a woman, mid-thirties, pushing a pram, too engrossed in her charge to be distracted. Satisfied there was no one who would recognise him, he went into the public toilet, shut the cubical door behind him and opened his bag. Inside was the suit he had worn the day before. Yesterday's funeral suit was today's business suit. Only a new blue and cream striped tie had been necessary to complete the transformation. In the absence of a coat hook, he laid the coat hanger carrying his jacket on top of the bag, trying to avoid unnecessary creasing as best he could. He then undid his school trousers and sat down to take them off before changing into their replacements. It was at this point that he suddenly became aware of the penis protruding through a roughly cut hole in the wall between his and the adjacent cubicle. He recoiled away from the invader, almost falling off the toilet as he did. His first inclination was to hurl a torrent of abuse at his anti-social neighbour but he couldn't risk creating a scene. Deciding to ignore it as best he could, he continued changing. His neighbour however was having none of that and Stevie couldn't help but watch as the offending member was waved frantically at him, becoming stiff in the process. As he refused to be ignored, Stevie decided to put him to use. Reaching down, he picked up the coat hanger and hung it on the "hook" beside him, which was the perfect height to keep the jacket off the floor. However, as it then began trying to hump its new best friend, Stevie knew he had to hurry. He stood up, zipped up the new trousers and quickly put his school ones in his bag. As the breathing from next door became heavier, he reached over and grabbed his jacket, just in time to save it from any embarrassing stains, and ran.

Upon reaching the opposite end of the park, he hid behind a tree and peered towards the toilet just in time to see a familiar face looking out of the gent's door, glancing around to see if it was safe to come out. Well, come out Mr Lewis certainly had. The English teacher had left the school abruptly six months earlier on "health grounds."

"Looks like you're still one sick fucker." Stevie watched Mr Lewis disappear in the opposite direction before hiding his bag behind a nearby bush and heading on his way.

At precisely 10.30, Stevie's taxi pulled up at the entrance to the bank. He paused for a second to check his reflection in the mirror. He looked young but sharp. Every inch the young entrepreneur he was about to become. Entrepreneurs see opportunities where others see only confusion. They didn't get it, but he did. And now he was going to give it to James Paterson, big time. He felt completely calm. Almost serene. A terrible crime had been perpetrated and it was his job to make sure the guilty would pay and the victims would be avenged. As a feeling of power swept over him, he smiled and opened the door. The bank was large and empty. Looking around, he checked out the CCTV situation. He counted 5, but they didn't factor into his plan. He quietly reprimanded himself for even looking, for looking guilty. A voice drew his attention.

"Can I help you," asked one of the tellers, a young lady, late twenties, brown shoulder length hair and very attractive. She smiled as he approached, a smile he reciprocated when he noticed her badge.

"Good morning Veronica, we spoke on the phone, Sebastian Smith to see Mr Paterson."

"Oh, yes...erm....you're... very young. Wasn't it for a business loan?"

"That's right. Richard Branson was onto his first million when he was twenty-two. Two of a kind, me and Richard."

"Twenty-two?"

"Yeh, I met him once. Smart guy. Gave me a few tips. Hope to return the favour someday."

"I'll tell Mr Paterson you're here," smiled the bemused teller.

"Cool" Stevie replied. Cool?!. Would Richard Branson say "cool"? A moment later he found himself being ushered into the manager's office.

"Please sit down Mr Smith," he said, eyes fixed on the paper work in front of him.

"Would you like tea or coffee?" asked Veronica.

"No thanks, I'm fine," replied Stevie. He looked around the drab, cluttered room, its walls punctuated by dust-covered scenic paintings, hanging off-level, littered with folders and scattered files. It was an office that had reached middle age and just let itself go.

James Paterson raised his head and made eye contact with his client. The practised smile he'd put in place dissolved as life slammed on the brakes, whip lashing his mind, bringing it to a stunned halt. As the colour drained from his face, the adrenaline being dumped into his bloodstream jump-started him back to life, finally allowing him to speak.

"Well Mr Smith, em...I believe you wanted to discuss a loan."

Stevie paused for a moment, trying to lock onto the eyes darting amidst the sweating death mask opposite. "We both know that my name isn't Smith and that I'm not here for a loan."

James's last desperate hope of coincidence evaporated. Stevie watched the banker seem to shrink in front of his eyes, shoulders drooping, slumping into his chair as he simultaneously felt himself grow, sitting upright, breathing slowly and deeply, chest expanding.

"So, why are you here?" he asked, in a barely audible whisper.

Stevie's gaze finally locked with the brown, bloodshot eyes before him and he spoke firmly and evenly. "I'm here because of what you did. I'm here for the people you killed, and for the people whose lives you destroyed. I'm here to make you pay. I'm here to make sure the victims, your victims, get justice, get what's owed to them, owed to them by you-"

"Because of what I did?"

"Be quiet," snapped Stevie, startled by the audacity of the interruption.

"What about what you did?" James continued, ignoring his accuser.

"I said shut up!"

"You're the maniac who made me crash."

"Made you crash?! Was I in the car?! Did I grab the wheel?!"

"No, but you startled me."

"Startled you! You've got brakes haven't you? I assume you know how they work? Have you even passed your fucking test?"

"You're every bit as much to blame as I am. More so."

Stevie felt himself on the brink of exploding, his righteous indignation on the brink of overpowering him, but just in time, realising the risks of drawing attention to himself, he forcibly calmed himself down.

"I'm not here to listen to your pathetic attempts to avoid accepting responsibility for your actions. As someone who kills innocent people and drives away, I expected nothing less."

"So what are you here for?" asked the banker wearily.

"I've already told you. I want justice."

"So why come here? Why aren't you at the police station?"

"The way I see it, there's two options. Option one, I do like you say. I go to the police, tell them the whole story and you pay for your cowardly murderous actions with some serious jail time, maybe for the rest of your miserable life. Or, there's option two.

"Which is?" He asked, the penny beginning to drop.

"You pay compensation."
James leaned back in his comfortably tattered old armchair and let out a quiet chuckle. "Oh I get it. Blackmail. All that bollocks about victims and justice, but you just want some money," he grinned, confidence rising.

"Compensation! Do you think you should just get away with it? Scott free! Is that what you think?"

"If you wanted justice, you would have gone to the police."

"Listen you fat fuck, I'm doing you a favour here. This way you stay out of jail and the two kids you orphaned get some financial assistance, which should also ease your piss poor excuse for a conscience."

"And what if I refuse? What are you going to do, eh? Because let's face it. Option one was never really an option anyway, was it? You stand to lose as much as me. You caused it in the first place and-"

"Stop trying to weasel out of it, ya cunt. You drove them off the road. Then you fucked off without calling an ambulance. You did that. Do you deny it?"

James paused for a moment.

"It's your word against mine. Where's your proof, eh?"

"Well I'm sure the cops will love to have a look at your car, for starters."

"I don't think you'll get too far with that one, sonny. My car was in an unfortunate accident the other day. Stupid dog ran out in front of me. Wrote the thing off. Maybe you'd like to read the police report," replied the smiling banker.
Stevie was silenced, but only for a moment.
"Maybe they'd like to have a look at some pictures. Great things camera phones. The resolution you get now. Amazing," lied the resurgent Stevie.

"You'll still get done for it too. You'd have to say you were there too. Why are you just reporting it now?"

"It's not my phone, officer. I only just found it. I looked though the pictures to see if I could find something to identify its rightful owner, to return it."

"For a reward no doubt."

"Well, when I stumbled across these horrifying images, I remembered the story in the papers and of course I contacted you straight away." James Paterson slumped back in his chair, too worn out to pick holes in Stevie's threadbare improvisation.

"The baby faced assassin, eh? I can't believe I'm being blackmailed by a fucking school kid."

"I'm twenty-two."

"Twenty-two my arse. I've got rashes older than you. Not as nasty though." He stared into the youthful eyes across the desk and saw no mercy.

"How much?"

"I thought you'd never ask." Smiled the baby face.

Ten minutes later a smiling Stevie emerged from the manager's office. Heading towards the door he turned his head, catching Veronica's eye. As she smiled he paused momentarily, before turning and walking slowly towards the curious teller, giving her his best movie star smile.

"Hi Veronica."

"Hi Sebastian," she replied, slightly unnerved.

"Listen, if you've nothing planned, how about coming out with me on Saturday night?"

"Eh, sorry, but I've got plans Saturday."

"Oh. Boyfriend?" he asked, fishing for information.

"Girlfriend, actually."

"You're gay?"

"I'm afraid so."

Stevie thought for a moment, processing the information. "I don't suppose wearing a dress would sweeten the deal? A little black number? I'll even shave my legs. Can't say fairer than that?"

She smiled, unsure whether to be amused or insulted but willing to give him the benefit of the doubt.

"Still a no, I'm afraid, but better luck with your business."

With that he turned and left, smile still intact.

CHAPTER 20

James Paterson slouched back in his tattered old leather chair, feeling pretty tattered and old himself. He stared blankly at the wall in front of him. All fear, anger, confusion, debate and rationale were spent. All that was left were the mental and physical collapse of surrender. Stevie had demanded a million pounds. A figure too absurd to be taken seriously, but Stevie was in no mood to be taken anything less than seriously. An explanation that a branch manager's salary made millionaire status the same distant fantasy for him as anyone else made little impression. The revelations of his wife's financial excesses, and how they had left him with barely a pot to piss in, even less so. No, in Stevie's eyes bank managers had access to vast fortunes, and a vast fortune he would have. The victims, with whom he would share the compensation, deserved no less, he declared. As the penny dropped that he was not being asked to empty his pockets, but to become a bank robber, James realised that the life he had known was over. He turned to what intellectual horsepower remained available to him and after some negotiation he managed to convince Stevie that the figure of one million pounds was fantasy. The most they ever had on the premises was around two hundred thousand, and that was the best he could do. However there did remain a rather obvious problem. Not getting the money out. That he could do. Getting it to Stevie, again no problem. No, the problem was how the hell option B was any more likely to keep him out of jail. Not his problem, Stevie had replied, though he had offered to take his family hostage at knifepoint to assist with that. The offer was quickly declined by an alarmed shake of the head. He was then given a deadline of one week and a mobile phone number to call when he had the money, before his teenage tormenter left, smiling and satisfied.

Two days later James found himself slouching once more in a leather armchair. This one however was barely a week old, purchased as part of a suite selected by his wife as the centrepiece of her latest interior design project. The suite it replaced, purchased barely 18 months earlier priced at just over £2,000, now sat in a charity's warehouse until its new needy recipient was identified. Jane Paterson sat opposite him, lounging on the settee watching a soap opera in glorious 52" HD.

"James?"

"Yes?"

"Do you think the TV's too big for the room?"

James clenched his teeth. "It's a bit late for that, eh," he snarled. "I told you it was too big."

"The TV's fine, I love it."

"Good."

"I'm only saying." She paused. "Maybe we need a bigger living room?"

"What!?" he exclaimed in disbelief.

"I'm just saying. I mean we've been in this house for five years now; maybe it's time to move. Somewhere bigger. The girls are getting older now. They really should have their own en suite bathrooms."

"You must be f-"

At that moment, Popsy and Flopsy, or Felicity and Carmel to use their real names, burst into the room, jumping up on the arms of the chair either side of their agitated father.

"Dad, Annie's got a new laptop, way better than mine, can I get a new one. Pleeeease, you'll be the best dad ever," pleaded Felicity, head tilted in mock cuteness.

"Me too dad, me too," echoed her sister.

"What? But you only got the ones you have at Christmas. They're only six months old for Christ's sake!"

"James, don't talk to them like that, they're only asking."

"Please dad, Annie's is so much better, it can-"

"No!" interrupted the exasperated dad.

"That's not fair! I hate you! I hate you!"

"So do I!"

The twins exited as quickly as they had entered.

"You can be such an old meanie," muttered Jane contemptuously, eye's returning to the TV soap, letting her disapproval linger until she decided he'd suffered enough.

As the TV frothed in the background, James Paterson stood up and left the atmosphere behind. He'd decided he'd suffered enough.

CHAPTER 21

Four days later, Stevie sat at the breakfast table, playing with two Weetabix in the bowl in front of him. As the days passed he'd grown more and more agitated by the lack of communication from his reluctant partner in crime. From his pocket he slipped the mobile phone he'd purchased specially, checking for texts. For the third time that morning he was disappointed. He tried reasoning that he had given the asshole a week so there was still plenty of time left, but he'd expected….he didn't really know what he'd expected; he just wanted to get on with it. Waiting was killing him, but he reasoned that expecting someone to hurry into turning their life upside down was maybe expecting too much. Maybe he was still figuring out how to get away with it. Good luck with that one, he thought, still not fully understanding the negative response to his kidnap ploy. It seemed perfect. Sure, they'd be shook up a little; maybe he'd have to give him a cut of the dough. Just a little, though. Buy his wife a new pair of shoes. He smiled for a second and then got on with the business of anger management. Truth was, he wasn't managing very well.

He thought about calling him at work, to see what the fuck he was playing at, but decided against. Don't panic, don't raise suspicions, stay off the radar. He'd already raised his profile too high with the lovely Veronica, making an impression, no doubt. He'd been stupid, but hopefully she wouldn't make a connection to the events about to unfold. No, he'd given him a week and a week he would have. And then...Well that was another problem altogether. What if he called his bluff? If he decided against going through with it? What then, because the truth was he had no real evidence. He could call the cops, anonymously of course. Tell them he saw the crash; give them a description of the car, registration, description of the driver, then hang up. But what evidence was there? The smart cunt had got rid of the car as a piece of evidence, which left fuck all. And what if Mr Wanker banker decided to turn the tables and tell them he was being set up and black mailed? He didn't know his name, but he could give a good description and knew he was a friend of the deceased's family. They'd find him easily enough. And he'd given him a phone. A phone with his finger prints on it. What if the cops told him to ring him and record it? Or arrange a meeting and get him to wear a wire and bust him on the spot. Panic grew with every movie plot he could think of. What the fuck had he started? But wait, the prick thought he had pictures, so as long as he believed that, and he seemed just convinced enough, he wasn't going to risk involving the police. No. He just had to be patient. He took a mouthful of cereal, chewing slowly, deep in thought.

Just then his mum, who'd gone out for cigarettes, returned and came into the kitchen. "You'll never guess what I've just heard, Son."

"Mmm," mumbled Stevie disinterestedly, chewing the same mouthful over and over.

"I was talking to Ellen at the shop. She says the manager at the bank in Woodstown's ran off with all the money."

"What?!" exclaimed Stevie, in a spray of wheat and semi skimmed.

"She said the manager of the bank ra-"

"What bank?!" he shouted at his startled mother, already knowing the answer.

"Eh, I think she said the Royal bank of-"

"Bastard!"

"No, Scotland. What are you so upset about, you don't have an account there unless you've been holding out on yer old mum. Is that it? You got a wee fortune stashed away? Saved up all your pocket money," she laughed.

"Fuck no. Don't be daft. Fucking bankers eh. Shoot the fucking lot of them!" replied Stevie, stunned.

"You're right there, Son." she smiled. "But mind the language, eh? I don't know where you get it from? Not Tommy, that's for sure."

"Yeah, a right fucking mystery."

"Ya cheeky wee bastard," yelled Margo, hand raised. Slowly she lowered it and both sat silently for a few moments staring blankly at the table. "Fancy a cuppa?" She asked.

"Yeah, ta." Sneaky bastard, he thought to himself still in disbelief. Who'd have thought it?

What greed drives people to do. "What about his family?"

"Eh? What family?"

"The banker's. Did they run away too?"

"No, that's what makes it even worse. They had no idea. First they knew was when the police turned up at their door. Apparently they were in a right state. Unless they're just acting. You never know with some people."

It looked like hanging onto his life was the last thing he wanted, and Stevie had just given him the push he needed to do something about it. A part of him almost admired Paterson's action. The other was pissed off at the loss of a fortune. But maybe it had all been pie in the sky. Not to James Paterson it wasn't, his inner voice chipped in. It still left Tommy and Susie in the shit though. Where was their money going to come from? Tommy had been expected to go to university. Who would look after Susie? Sure, they'd get benefits, student loans. Susie could come into theirs after school. It would be a struggle, though. He felt anger start to build again. He'd really wanted to help them out. Share the money with them, even though he wasn't the one who killed their parents. But, if only.... The saddest words in the English language. And also the most pointless. He couldn't spend his whole life afraid to go out and enjoy himself, just in case some nutter drunk driver crossed his path. It happened, and it can't be changed. But he had to try and do something.

"There you go, Son."

"Thanks ma."

"You're welcome," she paused for a moment. "I've got something to talk to you about."

"What's that?" He enquired suspiciously.

"How would you feel about Tommy and Susie moving in here?"

As Stevie's face lit up, she had her answer.

CHAPTER 22

Six months later. New Year's Eve.

Margo stopped mid-sentence, momentarily distracted. Over the blaring music, chatter and cackling, her ears picked up a faint knocking. She smiled and raised her left hand in a "be right back" salute, then made her way to the front door. As the party atmosphere dimmed behind her, the knock, knock turned to thump, thump. Now slightly irritated, she jerked the door open. In front of her, a startled Hughie backed up a step, his primitive percussion playing abruptly halted. They both stood silently for a moment, Margo still irritated by the assault on her door, Hughie, eyes darting all around, nervous, off balance. Resplendent in Crombie overcoat, silk scarf, and Italian loafers, he was all dressed up, but unsure if he had somewhere to go.

"Eh, good evening my dear and how you are this fine, lovely, eh… I hope you don't mind my…I'm not selling anything, with me dressed up like this. I haven't had this coat on since, eh…Henley Regatta, yes…mmm.. 1974. What a day that was, beautiful…Or was it Royal Ascot? The Queen was there, don't you know? A fine woman. A fine, fine woman. Beautiful, as indeed are you, not that you are as old her Majesty of course, well maybe in 1974 and you now…. Fine wines, you and the queen. Lots of fine wines at Henley…not at Royal Ascot though. Brandy at the races. Hip flask. Lovely. Not the queen though. She didn't have a hip flask. I had a hip flask. She was lovely though. Maybe Philip had a hip flask. Wouldn't be surprised. I'd drink too if I had a nose like his. Ugly bugger. He was Greek you know, probably still is, like Nana ...Mascara. Ugly woman. Remember her? Looked like Buddy Holly in a frock. Not as big a frock as that other Greek bugger. What's was his name...Denis Roussos or something. Good knows what goes on under that marquee he wears. He's a dog lover I believe. I bet he's lost a puppy or two under there...Can you hear bells? I can. I hear bells all the time. Chiming. Nursery rhymes, usually. I love nursery rhymes...and Motorhead. Do you like Motorhead my dear? Ugly buggers, every last one of them. Loud too, till I started going deaf. Quieter now....still ugly...bloody ugly. Pardon my French dear. I hate the French...I hope I haven't...."

"Oh for fuck's sake, shut up and come in you daft old cunt!"

"Ah my dear, such kindness, only if you're sure, I don't mean to impose...I was only passing...such a kind invitation. Please accept this bottle of fine wine as a token of-"
Reaching the end of her patience, she grabbed the bag of drink in one hand, and with the other, grabbed Hughie by the collar and propelled him head first down the hall.

"I'll stick this in the kitchen, party's in there. Don't steal anything."

Hughie slowly got to his feet, gladly accepting the wall's offer of support. Reaching into his pocket, he pulled out his trusty hip flask, unscrewed the lid, took a shot of its gut-rot cargo, winced, and tucked it safely away. Time to see what the natives had brought.

Inside the party was in full swing and had already suffered its first casualty. For reasons known only to himself, Sidney White from number 15, a lover of all things Olde English, had decided to come dressed as a Morris dancer. Having tried to whisk Margo away to join him in his merry dance he now lay slumped in the corner, knocked unconscious by a single blow to the head from his own pole. Freed from embarrassment, Mrs White thanked Margo profusely, relaxed, and enjoyed the company of a triple whiskey.

In another corner, Tommy sat and watched like a zoologist observing the behaviour and social patterns of some new species. Beside him, Stevie drank Vodka straight from the half bottle he had hidden in his pocket, its effects kept at bay for the moment by the two lines of amphetamine sulphate he'd hoovered thirty minutes earlier. Both knew most of the people there. An assortment of neighbours, friends, relatives and passing chancers. Neither Stevie nor Tommy had invited anyone. It wasn't that kind of a party. New Years at Margo's were strictly old school affairs. Besides, most of their friends were sitting at their own version, making the most of the opportunity to get drunk with the silent

acquiescence of their parents. It was Hogmanay,
after all. Stevie turned to Tommy and silently
offered him the bottle. Since his parent's death,
he'd not touched a drop of alcohol or drugs. He'd
been plagued by guilt that somehow that awful
event was punishment for choosing to stray from
the straight and noble path of his parents, to take
a few faltering steps on the wild side. He still
suffered flashbacks to the crippling terror and
madness of that night, pain he hid from the shell
of his sister. But maybe it was time for a new
start. Taking the bottle, he took a long swig and
passed it back to Tommy. It was Hogmanay after
all. The two friends smiled and embraced.

"I know it's been a shit year for you mate. I'm
sorry, I really am. But you've got to try and move
on."

"I know, it's just been so...with Susie being...It's
hard mate, really bloody hard."

"I know. I know. Well, no, I don't know. How
the fuck can I even begin to know what it's been
like? What you've gone through. But listen, look.
I know I haven't been there for you. I've been a
shit mate. I know that-"

"Look forget about-"

"No wait, wait man listen. I have, I've been a
shit mate. I'm sorry, I just didn't know what to
say...do...so I did fuck all...great mate, eh?"

"You-"

"Listen, I have. I've been shit, but that's going to
change. I'm goin to do everything I can for you
and Susie. Anything you want, need, name it, it's
done. I mean it. No fucking kidding."

Tommy smiled and took another shot from the bottle. He knew he had some catching up to do.

"Aw fuck, here we go," said Stevie with a wry smile.

"What?" asked Tommy, turning around to investigate.

The what was Margo, whiskey bottle in one hand, Karaoke machine in the other.

"Alright ladies and genulmin. Time fur the singers," slurred the inelegantly wasted Margo. She struggled for a while, untangling the nest of viper cables, trying every permutation of connections before stumbling, literally, on the correct match. Meanwhile the singers started to warm up, discreetly humming scales, coughing up lumps of tar and mucus washed down with a final shot of their particular poison. Discreet glances shot across the room to check out the state of the opposition. Anticipation grew. Then the karaoke display appeared on the screen.

"Right we're off," yelled the hostess. "Who's up first?"

Over the years a pecking order had built up, with everyone more or less knowing their place on the bill. First up was category one. The enthusiastically tone deaf who couldn't sing for shit, didn't care and gave everyone a laugh. This year, as with most years, the opening act was Uncle Bill and Auntie Cathie. After some consideration they decided, as they had for the last ten years, to go with the Sonny and Cher evergreen "I Got You Babe". However, for those ten years they and the others had sung unaccompanied. This was the karaoke machine's first outing, but for Uncle Sonny and Auntie Cher it may as well have stayed in the box. Ignoring the backing track, they gazed deep into each other's eyes, oblivious to everyone and everything as they proclaimed love and devotion, reaching the chorus about ten seconds after the backing track had left. As the song went on, the two lovers held on to each other as much for support as affection, like a pair of old Zimmers. Then, as the song reached its finale the audience, who had been waiting in the wings, burst in.

"I...goooot yooouu baaaabe!"
Everyone cheered, smiling as the couple kissed, roaring as things got a bit passionate.

"Get a room you two!"
Auntie Cathie smiled, blushing as she re arranged her dentures, led back to her seat by Uncle Bill, now very much in the mood for some loving.

An assortment of mice-turned-lions took it in turn to bring their fantasy to life, each convinced that they would succeed where the others had failed, clapping rivals with a faint air of smugness. Between turns, Tommy scanned the room trying to gaze into the souls of these people he'd lived amongst all his life yet had never really understood, whose lives had seemed empty. Yet as he sat there, puffed up by his own conceit, everywhere he looked people were smiling big beaming smiles. None more so than Uncle Bill who sat watching the entertainment with a large malt whiskey in his left hand and his right up Auntie Cathie's skirt. Tommy sat transfixed 'til the hypnotic spell was finally broken by Margo's bawling baritone.

"The minute you walked in the joint."

As she bumped and ground her way through Shirley Bassey's finest hour, Tommy turned to check Stevie's reaction. Instead of the expected embarrassment, Stevie was grinning with.... pride. He turned to Tommy, singing along, handing him a bottle of wine he'd liberated earlier. Gulping greedily, Tommy joined in, cheering as Margo's finale met with a favourable response from Hughie.

"Come here ya beauty! "he roared, burying his face between Margo's breasts, shaking his head from side to side, Margo cackling madly as she pulled his head in tighter.

Then an almost reverential quiet descended on the Karaoke stage, attention turning to the small balding man who had successfully blended into the background for the previous hour. Now a faint smile appeared as he became aware that it was his moment to shine, but like all stars...

"It's time for the chairman," yelled one voice.

"Yeah, the chairman of the board!"

"Alright Frank, up you get and show them how it's done!"

"Oh no, no, another time," replied Frank, sporting a suitably modest smile.

"Come on Frank, give us a song."

"Maybe later, let someone else have a go."

"Anyone else want a go?!" yelled Stevie, calling his bluff.

"Ok, I'll do it, I'll do it!" blurted Frank, voice tinged with panic at the thought of missing his moment. So up he got, the one, the only, Mr Francis Albert Sinatra. (Real name Ted Dobbs). His anticipation had been building from the very first sight of the karaoke machine. He'd watched as the amateurs crashed and burned. No amount of accompaniment and echo could save them. But now it was his time. Not just the voice, but a full big band behind him for the first time. He'd always been good, but now in full Rat Pack mode he was going to take it up a notch and he'd take them all with him.

"This is for all the dames," he winked, centre stage. "How about Come Fly With Me? Margo, can the band swing with that?"

"I'll jist go an have a word with the conductorer," slurred Margo, squinting as she worked her way down the track list.
As she did, Frank discovered a technical problem of his own. Normally singing unaccompanied, he did so with a cigarette in his left hand, scotch on the rocks in the right. But now there was a microphone to hold. Three props, only two hands. A puzzle of rubix cube proportions. He could do without the mic, just turn the track down, but this was his chance to do it for real. No Scotch? No Smoke? Frank would spin in his grave. Beads of sweat began to break out on his forehead. Then, as Margo started up the band, with relief came his epiphany. With microphone in his left hand, cigarette and scotch in right, he came in right on cue.

"Come fly with me, come fly, come fly away." He sang, cigarette pointing the way to their swinging destination. "If you can use some exotic booze." He smiled, eyes turned to the amber glass clinking in his hand. "There's a bar in far Bombay."

He felt the music's power fill him like never before. No wonder Frank never really retired. It may not be the Tommy Dorsey orchestra, but it was intoxicating.

As the second verse approached, booze references over, he reluctantly jettisoned the scotch. This allowed snapping of the fingers, upping the ring a ding ding as he lost himself in his performance. As Tommy and Stevie watched, they looked at each other and nodded. They too felt the power of Frank. "No fuckin bad, eh?!" declared Stevie.

"Not fucking bad at all." Tommy had to agree. Working the crowd, the final "Pack up, lets fly awaaaaaaaaay!" soared, ending the long last note in perfect synch with the boys in the band. As the room roared and applauded he bowed and made to sit down, but then, with a display of theatrical reluctance even James Brown would have been proud of, he returned to give the fans what they wanted. Moments later, a sombre hush filled the room out of respect for the anthem to which they all aspired.

"And now the time is near..."

Tommy watched as everyone in the room simultaneously lowered their gaze to the floor, each trawling over the memories and merits of their life thus far, with mistakes acknowledged but too few to mention. But then the sombre mood was jolted by the breaking of the cardinal rule.

"I did it my way," wailed Stevie, though with no trace of mockery or malice.

Piercing stares stopped him dead, before returning to further introspection.

"One singer, one song, Son," whispered Margo. Stevie nodded silently. As the song reached its stirring climax, eyes were once again raised, the final "Myyyy waaaaaaaaaaaaaaaaay!" bringing sage-like nods of satisfaction and applause. As he finally retook his seat, smiling broadly, Stevie slid across the carpet towards him.

"Sorry to interrupt there, mate, I just got carried away."

"That's ok son, it's just... to sing that song, well, you need to have lived, you know? To have experienced life," explained Ted, who'd never left the country and had been a milkman for all 42 years of his working life. But no doubt he'd delivered it his way.

"Right...nice one."

"It's nearly the New Year everybody! We nearly bloody well missed it!" yelled Uncle Bill, waving his now disentangled hand to catch every one's attention.

"Quick, has everyone got a drink!?" Margo shouted, surveying the room. "Get one, quick if you've not. Stevie! Go upstairs and get Susie son. Hurry up now everybody, it's nearly time!"

Stevie bolted upstairs to Susie's room and quickly knocked three times on the door before opening it. The room was empty. "Susie? Susie you there?" he enquired, more than a hint of concern in his voice.

"I'm here. What is it?" asked Susie.
Startled, Stevie span round to see Susie standing in his bedroom doorway.

"What are you doing in my room?" asked Stevie suspiciously.

"It's...quieter that's all," smiled Susie. "What is it?"

The sight of a smile on Susie's face startled him even more and ended any further questioning as he matched it with one of his own.

"It's nearly time for the bells. Coming down?" he asked gently, more hopeful than he had been earlier.

"Ok, I'll just get changed."

"No time Susie Q," Stevie informed her, grabbing her arm and whisking her downstairs."

"Wait, I don't have a drink," said Susie as they passed the kitchen.
She darted inside and before Stevie could stop her, had poured a large vodka.

"Whoah Susie...aw fuck it, it's New Year, but put some orange in it and don't tell mum," winked Stevie, just happy to see a little light at the end of what had been a long dark tunnel.

She did as she was told, and the two of them walked arm and arm into the living room just as the bells struck midnight.

"Happy New Year," bellowed everyone, before exchanging kisses and embraces. Even casualty corner was brought back into the fold, though minus any bells and sticks. Tommy looked around the room for a few moments before he caught sight of Stevie and Susie. Stunned, he gazed at a face he recognised as his sister. A face he hadn't seen for so long, and feared he never would again. Oblivious at first to the tears welling in his eyes, he wiped them away as he walked slowly towards her. Her smile widened as she saw him.

"Happy New Year, Tommy!" she yelled, throwing her arms around her brother's neck, wanting to hold on to him and this moment forever, feeling happier than she thought she'd ever feel again.

"Happy New Year, Sis," he whispered gently in her ear, holding her tight. "Happy New Year." After a while, he turned to the still smiling Stevie and pulled him in too."Group hug! Happy New Year, mate, and not before bloody time, I tell you, geez."

"I know, I know. Life goes on, mate and you've got to go on with it."

"A new year and a new beginning," smiled Tommy before they clinked their glasses together and all three were emptied.

"I hope that's orange," smiled Tommy, not really caring.

"Of course," lied Susie.

Till the wee small hours the drinks and laughter flowed in equal measure, until...

CHAPTER 23

The next morning Margos eye's opened gingerly, allowing her surroundings to slowly seep into her consciousness. Facing her was what appeared to be a child's finger painting on an orange wall. As her focus sharpened she let out a yell, pushing the object away from her. Falling victim to gravity and a hard-wood floor, the object moaned before rising in front of her.

"Aw fuck naw," sighed Margo.

In front of her stood the still dazed Hughie, naked but for a pair of heroically stained underpants, albeit not naked in the traditional sense, as a thick red pelt obscured any sign of skin.

"Cunt," he barked.

"You've had all you're getting o that, now fuck off ya smelly auld bastard," she shouted back, hurling his clothes at him.

He staggered into the living room, finding a little space amongst the empties and a wall to lean on. Dressed, he looked around for a moment until he found what he was looking for and put the half full bottle of rum into his pocket. Who'd know? He smiled to himself, before noticing the girl watching him from the other side of the room.

Waste not want not, eh?" said Hughie awkwardly, before making his exit.

Susie's eyes followed him out before returning to the wall in front of her. The buzz from the speed had long since departed, leaving only insomnia and the fading promise of a false dawn. She poured herself another vodka and drank. In the absence of sleep or peace, oblivion would do. Susie sat still; quiet, desperately holding on, but she knew it was only a matter of time before the emptiness was filled again with relentless torment. In her inebriated haze she had found brief solace, but she knew it had to end, and soon. Susie felt the waves of fear ready to break over her, but still she hung on, winning for the moment, but as she heard the house begin to waken, residents rising to headaches, dehydration and nausea, Susie felt the walls closing in again. As she rushed past him on the stairs, Stevie, with his eyes closed, barely registered the brush against his arm or anything else. Until he'd had a long drink of something cold and fizzy, washing down whatever pain meds he could lay his hands on, he was definitely not open for business. Food was out of the question. He just hoped the liquid (non-alcoholic), pills and the lining of his stomach would stay put.

At the top of the stairs, Susie was briefly distracted by noises, noises which only made sense when she passed the bathroom. A gap in the door revealed Margo sitting side saddle on the toilet, her chin cradled by the rim of the sink. What she had so enthusiastically consumed the night before, she was now just as desperate to be rid of, first from one end, then from the other, then both at the same time. Brief pauses were filled with breathless, prayerful promises.

"Aww God...never again."

God must be very busy on New Year's Day, thought Susie, before slipping silently into her room, unseen. Down-stairs, Stevie had made his way to the kitchen and now stood over the sink, wincing. His stomach had decided that it too wasn't open for business and had forcefully ejected the glass of diet coke, mainly through his nose, lodging a paracetamol tablet in his left nasal cavity. Clamping the right shut, he desperately tried to suck it back in, succeeding after a few attempts. Then, unsure whether to risk swallowing or just spit, he chose the latter and the pill rattled off the sink before disappearing down the plughole, soon to be followed by yellow bile, until his retches ran dry. Sitting on the edge of her bed, Susie cradled her head in her right hand sobbing softly. She made her own silent prayers. Prayers for a normal life, where only hangovers and bad boyfriends were hell. Where jeans that didn't fit and hair that wouldn't sit were a nightmare. If God was everywhere, couldn't He see her suffering? Feel her pain? Did He think this was fair? Had she really been so terrible? With no answers, she lay back exhausted.

As she felt herself sober up, the fear of fear gripped her. She darted through to Stevie's room, quickly opening his bottom drawer. Inside, beneath tee shirts and some other clothing were a few old video boxes. Knowing where to look, thanks to an open door and a moment's indiscretion, she opened up 'The Godfather', hoping for an offer she couldn't refuse. She got it. In the box was a plastic bag containing about thirty little round tablets. Enough. She felt guilty about stealing from someone who cared about her, who, for all his flaws, had shown her nothing but friendship and recently a shoulder. But she'd had enough. The light at the end of the tunnel was a lie, an illusion. Just another joke from a God at best uncaring, at worse, cruel. Well, she wasn't playing His torture games anymore. She started to put the empty box back but changed her mind, tossing it on the bed. Stevie at least deserved the truth. She then walked quickly and silently back to her room and changed. With the plastic bag in her pocket, she crept out onto the landing and stopped for a moment. Tommy. How could she just leave him, with no goodbye? She thought about looking in on him one last time, but what if he was awake? She could write a note. And say what? No one could understand. She had to just go, get away for now at least from memories of the past and from reminders that the past was all they had. This way it would be one less burden for Tommy to bear. So leave she did, silently, past the debris.

CHAPTER 24

Tommy's burden grew as the weeks turned into months with no sign or word from his vanished sister. How could she have done it, he had wondered so many times, just disappeared, no goodbye? How could she have been so thoughtless, so cruel....and how tormented must she have been? Every day he wondered what she was doing. Was she safe? Happy? Every day ground him down. Even starting university couldn't entice him to look forward. He'd only decided to pursue it out of respect to his parents who'd always encouraged him in that direction. But any excitement or anticipation had been replaced by cold duty.

Stevie however, had decided that the best strategy to mend Tommy's broken heart was to get him completely hammered and have as much nameless, shameless sex as possible. Would it work? Never one to let such details get in the way of a good night out, Stevie just wanted Tommy to see he cared, and if he got pissed and screwed senseless at the same time, all the better.

"You nearly ready? ... I'll meet you at the end of the road in ten minutes." Putting the phone down, Stevie walked towards the front door, stopping in front of the mirror for a moment to admire the view. In his new Armani shirt (fake) and even newer haircut he looked sharp. It was a cold night out but he didn't want to spoil the aesthetic with some shitty old coat. He smiled then braced himself.

"Fucking hell," he winced as he stepped out. For a second he questioned his sacrifice, but remembering the brown duffle coat alternative he jammed his hands in his pockets and sucked his lips in to spare them from frostbite, confident he'd have need of them later. As he walked, he checked his pockets. Money in the left, condoms in the right. The last thing he wanted was to pull out a pile of condoms at the bar. Having a packet of rough riders land in your cocktail would probably be considered forward by most young ladies. "All present and correct, now where's, T?" He asked himself, looking around. Tommy, who'd been visiting his Aunt, was nowhere to be seen. "Fuck's sake," he muttered to himself, rubbing his hands together. Just then Tommy appeared over the hill. "Hurry up for fuck's sake, I'm fucking freezing!"

"Tough shit," Tommy whispered to himself, smiling and slowing down a bit, snug as the proverbial bug in his new quilted coat. A sleeping bag with sleeves. "No coat?" asked Tommy as he approached, smiling.

"Some of us are prepared to sacrifice comfort for style," replied Stevie, teeth chattering like castanets, but with no sign of an 'ole" anytime soon.

"Yeah, blue really suits you."

"Fuck off!"

So off they set, Stevie desperately trying to get Tommy to hurry, Tommy unresponsive. As they turned the corner they both suddenly tripped, landing hard on the frozen tarmac.

"What the fuck!?" shouted Stevie, barely getting his hands out in time to break his fall.

As the two of them turned and looked, anger turned to shock as they saw Hughie lying face down on the pavement, just outside his front gate.

"It's Hughie. Is he dead?" asked Tommy in hushed voice.

"Naw, I'm no dead!" roared Hughie, but you fucking will be if you kick me again."

"What are you doing down there, ya fucking old loony, I nearly broke my neck. Get yer silly arse up!"

"Ah cannae."

"Eh? Have you hurt yourself," asked Tommy, concerned once more.

"Naw, I'm stuck."

"What do you mean stuck?" asked Stevie, curiosity rendering him temporarily oblivious to the cold.

"I just lay down for a wee nap."

Tommy didn't know whether to laugh or.....just at that point Stevie made up his mind for him.

"Hahahaaaaa, fucking brilliant," roared Stevie.

By this point the dam of Tommy's concern could hold back the madness of it no longer and he joined in with Stevie's roaring laughter.

"Aye, have a good laugh the pair of ye, an auld man freezing to death. Very funny ya pair 'o bastards, ye."

Gradually the laughter began to subside.

"He's got a point. Let's get him up," said Tommy kneeling down to get a closer look. "It's his beard; it's frozen to the pavement!"

This set Stevie off again, laughing so hard, he slipped, falling on top of the prostrate Hughie.

"Get off me, ya wee poof."

Stevie struggled to his feet as quickly as he could. "How are we going to free him? Have you got scissors or a knife in the house?"

"You're no cutting ma beard!" wailed the old man

"Do you want to die?" asked Stevie.

"You're no cutting ma fucking beard!"

The two boys stood silently and thought for a moment.

Two minutes later, Hughie arose shakily to his feet through a cloud of steam, beard defrosted and intact.

"Thanks boys."

"No problem," replied Stevie, zipping up his fly.

"Let's keep this between us though lads eh?"

"Don't worry about it Hughie, best laugh I've had for ages," said Stevie. "Away into the house and heat yourself up."

"And maybe a shower wouldn't go amiss," suggested Tommy.

"Eh? No, no. I was just on my way out. See you boys later."

"What? Don't you think you should wash your...."

As the steam dispersed, the boys watched stunned, as Hughie wove his way in a mainly forward direction along the road.

145

"That's you in 30 years," laughed Tommy.
"Fuck off!"

CHAPTER 25

As they approached the canopied entrance to the local hotspot, "Coco's", Tommy's nerves began to unravel. The crowd waiting outside seemed to get bigger with every step, all there to witness his complete and very public humiliation. Three little words tossed in his direction with the casual delivery of a jazzman, but the devastation of a hand grenade. "Not tonight, son". It meant; "your night's over, you are not cool, and I want everyone to know it." As they entered the milling crowd of the desperate and the damned, they caught god's eye.

"Stevie, my man!"

Tommy looked behind for the other Stevie.

"Alright mate, how's it going?" replied the only Stevie in the vicinity.

"Good man, good."

Stevie turned and pointed at the baffled Tommy. "He's a mate."

"Good enough for me, in you go, have a good one."

Tommy floated in on a cloud of cool. "Who's that?" Asked Tommy, in almost reverential tones.

"I was wondering that myself, but then the penny dropped. He must be one of mum's...you know. One of the perks I suppose," said Stevie, with a wry smile.

"What you want to drink?" asked Tommy.

"Vodka and Red Bull. Double."

Tommy's heart hung heavier than his wallet. It was going to be an expensive night. When he returned, Stevie was checking out the action on the dance floor. Tonight was a Motown night, meaning good music, but an older clientele.

"Looks a bit grim, eh?"

"Not at all," replied Stevie. "It's grab a granny night. Things are looking up mate."

"How so?"

"Glad you asked. You see with the younger filly, even if she fancies you, she's going to make you jump through hoops before you get even a nibble. Yes, you can play it cool, but if she calls your bluff, you and your hard-on are taking the long lonely walk to wanksville."

"A dark and desperate place."

"My thoughts exactly."

"But no doubt you have a solution, or at least a glimmer of hope for us mere mortals?"

"Doubt not, hope is at hand. Can you give me an amen?"

"Amen brother."

"Amen indeed. Hope comes in the form of the more mature lady. A lady who knows her own mind, who knows what she wants, what she needs, who isn't there to fuck about. Yes she's there with friends, all pretending they're just out for a laugh, a dance, a few drinks, but behind that facade of harmless fun, the sexual cauldron simmers away, waiting for magic to happen. Because at the end of the night, you pull, you're cool. And if you don't. Well you feel a little older, a little less desirable, a little more patronised...."

and a lot more desperate. And that, my friend, is where we come in."

"Us?"

"To help her in her time of need. To save her from humiliation."

"I never saw you as a knight in shining armour."

"I don't see many fair maidens either. But there is no fuck like a charity fuck."

"A charity fuck?"

"Yeh. Not only have they pulled, but they've got a toy boy. They're now the coolest girl in the class, and with that mixture of gratitude and teenage giggles revisited, well they're up for anything."

"Well?"

"Well, what?"

"On you go then, stud."

"Eh, later…wait till they're pissed….just to make sure."

Laughing, they both headed to the bar.

Even with Stevie's relentless energy, a joyous Motown soundtrack and some world class comedy dancing, Tommy couldn't quite shake the melancholic mist enveloping him. Susie was never far from his mind no matter how he tried to displace her. Truth was he didn't try very hard. He wanted her there, alive in his head at least, no matter what the unbearable reality may be. He didn't want to forget. He didn't want to give up on her, not even for an instant. The ache of not knowing, the torment of an imagination careering from one horror to another, no act too depraved, no outcome too bleak, no mercy. This was his cross, willingly borne but no less a struggle for that. Then, as if the DJ could read his mind, Smokey Robinson's high pitched, sorrow laden voice filled the room, "The Tracks of My Tears", followed by "The Tears of a Clown." Anthems to heartbreak telling him he wasn't alone, and tonight Tommy decided Mr Smirnoff could take some of the weight.

As the evening wore on, Stevie's efforts to get Tommy to participate in his lustful scheming had come to nothing. Every request, nudge or push was declined in favour of more anaesthetising drink. For all his earlier bravado, Stevie knew his master plan would be a lot easier executed as a pair. Girls didn't even go for a piss on their own, never mind going off alone with a stranger, and now as the first slow song of the night began he knew he didn't have much time. Ever the pragmatist, he decided he only had one card left to play.

"I know it's tough for you mate, but don't you think Susie would want you to have a good time. Come on up for a dance...for Susie. Eh? What'd you say?"

The Captain Caveman subtlety bounced off Tommy's drunken head.

"I'm not a fuckin dancer; you're the fucking dancer, the fuckin chancer. Up you go then super stud. Fuck them. Fuck them all."

"Easy Tommy, I'm just trying..."

"She's got some pair, eh?" Interrupted the distracted Tommy. "Look at the bangers on her. Bangers and snatch, breakfast of champions, eh? Ha ha ha," he slurred.

"Well go and get her then."

"Ok, I will. Fuck it! Look and learn Stevie boy, look and learn."

Tommy swaggered and staggered out to the dance floor, eye's fixed on the breasts that had captivated him. The breast's owner looked to be in her early fifties, tall, fat, (to be blunt), with dyed blonde hair. As she stood, ruing another wasted night, she saw a handsome young guy heading in what appeared to be her direction. Anticipation grew, but did she dare hope? Maybe he would just walk past her, so best to play it cool. But when he stopped right in front of her there could be no mistake. She smiled and tried to make eye contact, but his eyes were elsewhere. She waited for him to speak, until finally; "Hi, I'm Shirley," she yelled over the music. Tommy looked up; eye's quizzically trying to focus. "Can I squeeze them?"

As he struggled to his feet, his fellow revellers parted to form a guard of dishonour, sniggering and sneering as he made his way back the way he had come, head bowed, rubbing the red handprint throbbing on his left cheek. He looked around for Stevie and the nearest exit, but could see neither. Reluctantly, he looked back out onto the dance floor, wincing inside every time eye contact was made, however briefly. Then, as a forgettable 80's power ballad miraculously turned every Colin and Mary into Romeo and Juliet, he spotted Stevie dry humping his last throw of the dice. Her black satin mini dress strained to contain a figure with more curves than a curly wurly. Her hair was dyed, but shouldn't have been. But for now at least, he was the King and she was his Queen, and Tommy once again the busted flush. He searched around for an exit and found himself once again under the canopy.

"No luck tonight, then?"

Tommy turned and shook his head. The doorman, a girl on each side, smiled sympathetically. "Maybe next week, mate."

Tommy smiled wanly, turned and headed for home. As the fresh air hit him the effects of the alcohol, temporarily slapped out of him, returned. Steps grew heavier as he lurched onwards waltzing from side to side, walls and lampposts restoring his balance, a step back, then forward again, oblivious to the couple on the other side of the road, their pointing, their laughter. Autopilot was engaged for home and bed. Everything else could wait.

But Stevie had other ideas. "Tommy!" yelled a voice in the distance. To Tommy it could have been the moon. "Tommy!" Louder this time, but still glancing off its intended target. "Tommy!" Eventually Tommy turned to find Stevie standing just behind him.

"Why did you leave? I was looking for you."

"I thought you'd got off with someone?"

"I did, but I was trying to get someone for you."

"So did you just come away yourself?"

"Did I fuck! She's back there a bit. I ran on when I saw you. She'll be here just now."

"Oh."

"She's phoning her pal to see if we can fix you up."

"Oh...Right"

"Don't sound so excited!"

"Eh, I'm just a bit pissed."

"No fucking wonder, you were chucking them down."

"Stevie! Stevie!"

They both turned as a sea lion in stilettos waddled frantically in their direction.

"Ok, ok I know she's not up to much, especially in the light, but..."

"What's her friend like?!" interrupted Tommy, his voice more than tinged with panic.

"Calm down and sober up."

"I am fucking sober, the future Mrs McDaid's seen to that."

"Ha ha, very funny. I don't plan to be walking down the aisle with her tonight."

"Not in those shoes."

Stevie smiled. "Any port in a storm, as they say."

"Where are you going with her?"

"Back to mine. Mum's out, won't be back tonight."

"Who's she out with?"

"Dunno. Doubt if she does. Let's go."

They headed off in the direction of home.

"Stevie!"

"Hurry up!" he yelled back, not even turning his head.

A few moments later she caught up.

"You're an ignorant bastard, did you know that?" She yelled breathlessly.

"Yes. Yes I did."

"Are you not going to introduce me to your friend?"

"It's because he's my friend that I'm not going to introduce you."

"I'm Tommy."

"I'm Diana. At least you've got manners. Call me Di."

"I didn't think it was manners you were after. Did you get him fixed up?"

"No. Sorry Tommy, all my friends are going out with someone."

"Fuck. That's shit, eh? Sorry mate."

"Yeh, well, I'm a bit tired anyway."

"Tired? It's only twenty past two."

"Here, have some of this, it'll liven you up." said Di, producing a bottle of vodka from her handbag.

"Eh, I think I-"

"Don't be a lightweight, get it down you," she said with a smile.

Tommy unscrewed the top, took some into his mouth, waited for the gag reflex to pass, and then swallowed. Five minutes later, they opened the front door and headed for the living room.

"You got any wine Stevie?" asked Di?

"Yeh, probably. Red or white?"

"White. You got anything to eat? I'm starving."

"Yeah. Starving, I can see that. Don't want you wasting away in front of me."

"No need for that, I'm only asking."

"Phone a pizza, the menu's next to the phone. Get a big one, anything you want, just no anchovies. I fuckin hate anchovies."

"What about you Tommy?" she asked.

"Its okay, I'm not hungry."

Di passed the vodka back over to Tommy and picked up the phone. As she dialled, Tommy, with nothing better to do, took the opportunity to check her out. Stilettos and fishnet tights, or maybe stockings, yes, stockings, and that dress, it was almost up at her waist already, and-

"Enjoying the view?"

Startled, Tommy fixed his gaze on the first innocent object that came into view before looking up to see Stevie grinning.

"What?" he asked sheepishly.

"I saw you."

"Leave him alone."

"Oh, fancy a threesome, eh?"

"You should be so lucky," smiled Di.

"Here, have some of this," said Stevie handing the bottle of wine to Di.

"Trying to get me drunk? Haven't you got any glasses?"

"Glasses? Are you the Queen in disguise?"

She took the bottle and several gulps before passing it to Tommy, smiling flirtatiously as she did. "Where's the toilet?" she asked.

"Upstairs, to the right" replied Stevie.

When he heard her reach the top of the stairs, Stevie sat next to Tommy.

"I think she's up for it."

"Eh? Up for what?"

"A threesome. Looks like you're getting lucky after all, but I'm first ok, you can have slippery seconds. Maybe she'll give you a blowjob while I'm nailing her. I'll get her started, then you join in."

As the wine and vodka kicked in, Tommy felt himself turned on by the idea. Fuck it, why not he thought. "Sound," he smiled, taking another gulp of the wine before passing it back to Stevie.

"Bottoms up."

"Let's try that too," slurred Tommy.

As Di returned and sat on the couch, Stevie sat beside her.

"You want some of this?" he asked, offering her the wine. She took a drink, and then passed it back to Tommy.

"Now how about some of this." Stevie turned her head and kissed her, gently at first, then more roughly, pushing his tongue deep inside. She responded, glancing over towards Tommy, their eyes locking as Stevie unbuttoned the front of her dress, lifting her bra clear of its fleshy burden, sliding the dress over to expose her left breast to both him and their voyeur. He then sucked hungrily on the swollen nipple as Tommy grew more aroused, watching her as Stevie's left hand slid down to her thigh, moving inwards, upwards, lifting the skirt, revealing the tops of her stockings, until suddenly, eye contact was

156

broken, her hand abruptly stopping Stevie's hand in its tracks.

"What's the matter?" whispered Stevie.

"The time of the month."

"I don't mind."

"Well I do," she said, returning the expeditionary force to base camp.

Stevie sighed, then returned to kissing, treading water as his mind worked furiously on plan B. After a moment he slipped his left hand round her waist, and with as much subtlety as his raging hard on would allow, tried to coax her round on to her stomach.

"What are you doing?"

"Well, you've got a nice arse, why waste it? We're all grownups; you're not prudish are you?"

"No, but I have got four kids."

"So? They didn't follow you here did they?"

"Don't be stupid."

"So?"

"When women have kids, sometimes you end up with...you know?"

"No, I don't know."

"Trouble down there."

"What are you talking about?"

"Bum grapes." Clarified Tommy.

With a heavier sigh, Stevie recommenced kissing, cursing his luck, fondling the breast half-heartedly as he tried to salvage the situation. He softly stroked her cheek with his right hand, then her hair, then slowly moved his left hand up until he gently cupped her face in his hands. Making eye contact, he slowly ran his tongue over her lips. She smiled, rubbing and flicking her tongue against his. He smiled back, gazed tenderly into her eyes, and slid his hands slowly behind her head, applying a hint of downward pressure. A hint he hoped she would take. Tommy smiled, his drunken lust returning, but...

"What's the matter now?" asked Stevie, exasperated as plan C followed A and B down the toilet.

"Nothing."

"It must be something. There's nothing disgusting about it."

"I never said there was. It's not that."

"Well then, what's the problem?"

"If you must know it's these. Ok! Happy?!" Yelled Di displacing the dental plate with her tongue, before quickly replacing it.

"Every orifice a fucking adventure, eh?!" snapped Stevie.

She turned away sharply, her face red with embarrassment and anger. The room fell silent. All heads bowed, praying to be somewhere else.

"Look, it doesn't matter, babe."

Di smiled, misunderstanding.

"Just take them out," suggested Stevie hopefully. But hopes eternal spring had run dry.

"No, I bloody well won't take them out!"

"Why not?"

"Because I'll just feel...."

"What?"

"Old!"

"Don't be daft; you're in your prime!"

"Just leave it, ok?!"

"So why the fuck did you come here eh?"

"I thought we could talk, you know, have a laugh."

"Talk? If I want to hear a bird talk I'll buy a fuckin budgie! Look around. You see any packets of Trill lying around? Is that a faint tweet tweet I hear? No, it's not; it's the sound of my fucking night turning to shit."

"That's it, I'm going home." She said, rising to her feet.

"You're goin nowhere!" Snarled Stevie, pushing her back down.

Shocked and bewildered she looked at Stevie, then turned her head to Tommy, their eye's meeting once more, this time hers moistening, pleading. He slowly bowed his head, and then looking away, he stood up, paused, and swayed towards the living room door.

"Please." She whimpered.

He stopped and turned. The two friends stared at each other, tense and silent, unsure as to what happens next. Then the doorbell broke the silence.

"That'll be the pizza!" said Di nervously. "I'll get it."

Stevie's arm shot quickly across, blocking her escape. The doorbell rang again, followed by a knock.

"Stevie!" snapped the sobering Tommy sternly, eyes fixed on his friend.

Stevie blinked first and slowly removed his arm.

"Look, I was only messing about ok? Just get to fuck. No pizza for you, ya fat cow."

She grabbed her bag and dashed to the door, almost knocking the pizza delivery boy over on her way out. He turned and looked quizzically through the open door.

"Pizza? "enquired the teenager, tentatively.

"I think you're right Sherlock, well done you. Isn't it past your bedtime wee man?"

"Eight pounds fifty seven please."

"She's a bit heavier than that, probably got the age right though. That's some fuckin face you've got there eh? A pizza face. Do I squeeze yer spots for mayo?" Mocked Stevie cruelly.

The acned youth blushed as his eyes darted away from his tormentor.

"Here. Keep it." Stevie, now bored, handed over a ten pound note and took the box from his visibly relieved and speedily departing victim.

"And the meek shall inherit the earth," he muttered under his breath. "Still, at least we've managed to salvage something from the night, eh? I'm fucking starving."

"Me too" replied the drained Tommy, following him into the kitchen.

"Fucking anchovies!!"

CHAPTER 26

The next morning, Stevie shuffled into the kitchen, checked the kettle for water and clicked it on. Waiting, he turned and saw Tommy sitting quietly at the table. Exchanging barely discernible nods he turned away, staring intently at the kettle. When finally the watched kettle boiled he made himself a cup of black coffee, swirling the steaming ebony liquid round and round, watching his reflection, blowing repeatedly to cool, swirl, blow, round, round, blow, swirl, gaze, swirl, before inevitably taking his place at the tense, silent table. The only sound came from a fly buzzing around the room before it landed on Tommy's ear, lifting its leg to clean its eyes, relaxing, unthreatened, pausing before another short flight, perching on the rim of Stevie's mug, until overcome by the heat it once more buzzed through the sullen atmosphere as outside a car engine fired up, providing welcome respite, until once more all that could be heard was the shrill atmospheric whine of not quite silent silence only noticed in moments of stillness, but today unnoticed, buried beneath mournful, deafening, shame. They sat, unable to find words, giving up the search, resigned to their own silent screams. And then, returning from who knows where, what or whom:

"Morning boys, did you have a good night?"

"Ok," was all Stevie could muster.

"Did you meet any girls, eh? Is the washing machine going be working overtime on my sheets today?"

"No, no girls Margo."

"A handsome pair like you two? Are you gay or something, not that I'm one to judge."

"No mam, not gay, no girls, just a drink."

"You're awful quiet, the pair of you."

"Just hung over mam."

"Yeah, sore heads Margo."

"Well I'm goin to my bed for a bit, I'm knackered; some of us know what's what."

The pair sat silently, staring at their mugs, the tension of the previous night still thick in the air. Eventually telepathic agreement was reached never to speak of it, leaving Stevie to break the silence.

"Did you ever feel like you were going mad?"

"Eh?

"I just feel like I'm losing it. I'm either tired or wired. I'm sick of just getting wasted all the time you know? ...Nothing makes any sense."

"So what are you going to do with yourself?"

"How'd you mean?"

"Well, when I go to university?"

"Geez," he sighed. "I dunno. I need to do something, I don't want to just keep drifting ...idle hands, the devils playground and all that, but I don't want stuck in some dead end job either, getting told what to do all day just to make somebody else rich. If somebody treats me like a battery hen, I'll peck their fuckin eyes out."

"Have you looked for a job yet?"

"No, not yet. I don't know what I want, that's the problem. I only know what I don't want. I wouldn't mind being my own boss. An entrepreneur, know what I mean? It's just getting the idea."

"Yeah, that's the hard bit. Not fancy college?"

"Fuck no; I've had enough school, thanks. I...I Just need something to get me out of bed in the morning you know? To do something worthwhile."

"I know what you mean. What are we here for if not to save the world, eh? What about charity work?" offered Tommy.

"Eh? Me? The new Bob Geldof? Can you see it? No, me neither. I need to make some money, get a life. I don't want to be living here forever."

"My auntie was saying they were looking for people at Avon Park care home. Why not give them a call?"

"Care home? Wiping up piss and shit all day? Don't fancy that."

"Might open your eyes."

"That's what worries me. Na, don't think so."

CHAPTER 27

The Avon Park Retirement Community resided in a modern, clean, featureless building. Its antiseptic air reinforced a reputation for good hygiene, but any colour had been bleached out along with the germs. Its freshly painted, white, roughcast expanse was only broken by a scattering of UPVC windows, invariably locked, even on the hottest day. And hot it was when Stevie approached on his first day, already 15 minutes late for his 2 'til 10 shift. Opening the door and finding the reception deserted, he stood for a few moments awaiting the return of the beautiful Susan, a blonde, early twenty-something stunner who had led him to his interview two weeks earlier. After five minutes of studying the abstract art hanging around him, he grew tired of waiting and set off in search of life, preferably blond, with long legs and big tits. As he turned the corner he found himself in the residents lounge. At the far end of the room an older chap with a military bearing set about assembling the bingo equipment as if it were the rifle he'd stripped and re-built so many times a lifetime ago. Each part was laid out, inspected and cleaned as necessary before being fitted in place. To his left, a lady was busy arranging tables and chairs. Neither blonde nor long legged, she did however meet his third criteria. Unfortunately their location, hanging by her waist, rather spoiled the effect. As she was wearing a tunic, indicating some official capacity, he decided to approach, reading her name badge as he did.

"Excuse me, Senga; I'm looking for the supervisor."

"You're late," barked the woman, without looking up from the task in hand, "and its Mrs Black to you!"

"Eh. I'm-"

"Stephen McDaid. You're still late. The shift starts at two. Sharp!" she snapped, cutting him off.

"Right. Sorry. Are you the supervisor?"

"If I was, you'd be out the door." She stopped for a moment, looked him over and let out a heavy sigh.

"Come with me, quick!"

She scuttled off down the corridor like a frantic hamster, leaving Stevie behind in her wake, struggling to catch up, before finally stopping at a door in a dimly lit hallway somewhere near the back of the building. Pulling a key from her pocket, she quickly opened the door.

"Stay here," she commanded.

A moment later she emerged with a pale blue tunic, thrusting it into his hands. Blue for boys, pink for girls. How cute, he thought to himself, smiling.

"Put this on and let's get to work."

As they hurried back, Stevie put on the tunic, quickly realising it was tailored for the more generously proportioned care worker. "Excuse me but this is a bit big, can I get-"

"Stop moaning, it's fine, it's not a cat walk you know."

If I was a cat I'd bite your fat fucking hamster bitch head off, he thought to himself... very quietly.

"Go and get the cups and saucers from the kitchen and start setting the tables. Quick!"

"Fuck's sake," he muttered under his breath. After a few steps, he stopped. "Where's the kitchen?"

Prospects for long-term employment were looking bleak.

Come 3 O'clock, the first of the residents began to shuffle slowly into the main lounge, mostly under their own steam, though a few Zimmer frames provided support for the less able bodied. By about 3.15, the traffic had subsided, tea cups were filled (coffee was considered over stimulating) and eyes were down for the first number. The Sergeant Major pressed the start button and they were off. The numbers were exclaimed with military precision, with no time wasted on superfluous waffle about fat ladies, legs, or clickety-clicking. Stevie looked around at a room filled with everybody's and nobody's granny and granddad. Dim eyes, bored and vacant, peered half-heartedly from the grey or balding, wrinkled heads. Some looked at the numbers in front of them. A few even marked them off. Most, like the clock on the wall, were just passing the time, a sip of tea, a nibble (or suck) of biscuit helping to break the monotony.

By the time one of the few players had called house, Sarge had almost run out of balls. Relieved, he walked over and checked the numbers. Relief was short lived, however, when the numbers proved to be false. With only four numbers still to be called, the "lucky winner" had two of those marked off. He looked the winner straight in the eye. His years in the military had made him a pretty good judge of character. He could see through any malingering recruit trying to pull a fast one, but there was no penetrating the enigmatic smile of old Annie Smith. "We have a winner!" he yelled with enthusiasm as genuine as his hair. He handed over the pound coin, which was quickly deposited in a battered leather purse, and marched back to the podium. "Now then, ladies and gentlemen, game number two."

At 4 O'clock on the dot, Sarge began dismantling his equipment under the impatient gaze of the next turn. Once finished, Marion Caruthers huffily made her way onto the podium, followed by her accompanist husband Terry. Arranging her flowing, pastel shaded gown to best effect, she began some warm up vocal exercises while Terry adjusted his keyboard settings to provide a complementary but unobtrusive backing. He knew his place. As this went on, Stevie noticed several residents make some adjustments of their own, as hearing aids around the room were hurriedly turned to zero. After the first verse, Stevie reckoned diva of the deaf was an apt description, and exited stage left.

The residents of Avon Park were clean, well fed, and comfortable and Stevie swore he would never, ever end up in a place like it. Over the passing weeks he got to know the residents pretty well. Not just their needs, what they needed help with, what they could do for themselves and what pills they took, but more importantly what they enjoyed and didn't, their stories, what they thought , their families, who got visitors and who didn't. While there was some who were just moaning faced old cunts, most he grew to like. Decent people, who had lived for the most part, full lives. But as they had lost their independence, becoming an inconvenient burden, they found themselves discarded into the care of others, fed, watered and sheltered like dogs in a kennel. Most had regular visitors, sons, daughters, an occasional grandchild dragged along. But the smiles and hugs on arrival were all too soon transformed into guilt and shame as abandonment approached, leaving the spirit of those left behind a little bit more crushed and withered each time. Yet, as he watched this ritual repeated day after day, Stevie's cynicism was tempered by the simple question: Would he be any different? His pledges to the contrary left him unconvinced. These people needed 24 hour care, and he could walk away every night after his shift. Who was he to judge? But for the time he was there, he decided to at least try and make a difference.

Later that night, Stevie sat back on his bed watching TV as a generic US cop show played out its high speed drama, its muted soundtrack replaced by the Doors letting it 'roll, baby roll all night long'. A smile emerged as the E he'd taken earlier began to dissolve the frustrations and gloom built up over 8 hours of Avon Park. Looking after Weasel's stash was not without its perks. "Help yourself, just don't go nuts," he'd been offered as payment. Seemed like a good deal at the moment. As long as he was making money, Weasel wasn't one for stock checks. Stevie started to count them but gave up at 320. He reckoned about 1000. Weasel, having no wish to come within half a mile of Margo, who's detection he feared far more than any law enforcement, just called them off 100 at a time which Stevie delivered. When stocks were running low, a new batch appeared which Stevie picked up and hid under a floorboard in his room. As the E kicked up a notch, his view of Avon Park became less negative. He loved those old fuckers and he had to figure out a way to help them feel young again, to feel life could be worth living, even fun.

CHAPTER 28

Tommy looked down the line as the tracks disappeared into the horizon. He glanced at his watch then back down the line, chewing at nothing, trying to induce some moisture into his nerve-parched mouth. He glanced again at his watch. Mickey's big hand was at quarter past, his little hand at eight. The watch was a gift from his mum and dad on his twelfth birthday. Up until his fifteenth birthday it had never been off his wrist, except for battery replacement. Once adulthood came knocking however, it didn't seem too cool. But the previous day he had been looking for something else and had come across it. He'd held it warmly like an old friend and after a thoughtful pause put it back on. He vowed to keep it there as a constant reminder of his parents and actually, it looked pretty cool. But now it was a deliverer of bad news, a messenger of doom, of ill omens and disaster. It was 8.15 and the 8.10 was still not in sight. His first day at university started at 9.00 sharp. The train journey was 30 minutes. The university was 10 minutes' walk. This gave him 10 minutes to spare. But 10 minutes was now 5 minutes. Five fucking minutes, that's nothing. But that was 5 minutes if the train arrived now. He gazed hard into the distance squinting his eyes, as if that would turn them into binoculars. Nothing. He wondered how long it would take to reach the station once it came into view. Five minutes, maybe even 10? What if it's broken down, or been cancelled? Had he looked at the wrong part of the timetable? He cursed himself for being so stupid. He should have got the earlier train. Another half an hour would have given him plenty of time to settle in, relax. But no. Better to have another thirty minutes in bed eh, and get stressed out of his brain. Not such a fucking good idea now. But the truth was, he was dreading it, and staying in bed 'til the last minute at least delayed things. But now, having run out of last minutes, he looked at his watch again. Nearly 8.20. He looked again into the distance and this time saw, or thought he saw, just a dot. Squinting, willing, praying. The dot was getting bigger. He was sure it was. Squint harder. It was definitely getting bigger, but it wasn't getting bigger very fast.

"Put your foot down you stupid bastard, hurry up," he whispered under his breath, immune to the curious glances he was now attracting. Another look at his watch. 8.22. A bigger dot now. 8.23. He could actually make it out as a train. Finally at 8.26 the train drew to a halt. Tommy turned to his fellow travellers. "Fifteen minutes late. Bloody ridiculous. Supposed to be here at ten past eight! They just couldn't care less could they?" he muttered.

"It is ten past," replied a bemused older man, dressed for another day of hardcore drudgery.

"Eh? You're joking?" gasped Tommy in disbelief.

"No. No I'm not," he replied with a slight air of offence. The man held out his watch as confirmation.

"Geez," sighed Tommy. "Nice one Mickey." He shook his head and found a seat as the others paused, waiting till he had, making sure there was ample space between them and the madman with the Mickey Mouse watch. Eye contact and conversation were to be avoided at all costs. Tommy didn't notice and wouldn't have cared anyway. He was happy in solitude, unconvinced of the value of small talk. So they all sat, eyes fixed on the floor, remaining vigilant against accidental eye contact, knowing one unguarded moment could lead to thirty minutes of torturous drivel.

Other than some human traffic exiting and entering en route, the silence held, and at 8.40, or 8.55 if you're on lying bastard Disney time, the train pulled into Woodstown station. Tommy exited sharpish and walked as fast as he thought he could get away with, without looking as if he was desperately trying to contain something within his back passage. Soon he was out on the street, weaving between very pedestrian pedestrians, crossing roads more or less without incident, until, after eight minutes of power walking and only one near miss, he raced up the entrance steps and finally into the University of Woodstown. Degree in Media studies. Day one.

After some pointing in the right direction, Tommy took a seat near the rear of the classroom and looked around. His fellow students were a pretty ordinary looking bunch, not the bohemian gathering he'd anticipated. At the front sat a couple of desperate poseurs wearing hats, one a charity shop trilby, the other an absurd velvet beret. Having entered as strangers, the hats had gravitated towards each other in their libertine finery to unite in the secret truths only they knew and understood. But on the whole, no one would get a second glass. Across the other side of the class Tommy noticed the obligatory Peruvian goat herder's hat. Maybe on those cold, lonely Peruvian nights such a colourful display would guarantee some four legged fun with the goat of your choosing. In Woodstown you just looked like a twat. Near the front of the class slouched a James Dean look-alike in black leather jacket, jeans, white tee shirt, the hairstyle, the whole 'rebel without a cause' bit. Tommy had to admit he looked pretty cool, not like goat herder dude. He smiled to himself as he looked back over...but he was gone. To round up a missing goat no doubt. Or maybe..."oh God no!" He thought.

"Excuse me, is this seat taken?"

Tommy felt his worst fears about to be confirmed as despair consumed him, hindering the speedy construction of a convincing lie. Hell, any lie would do. Maybe bluntness would be more effective? He turned to get it over with, as Multicoloured earflaps and pom-poms dangled before him.

"Actually..." Tommy stopped breathing, mesmerised by the glistening green eyes of goat herder girl. His mouth opened in silent wonder, his mind knowing words to be futile, feeling instinctively that his life was now better.

"I'll take that as a no," she smiled back, sitting. "My names Katie."

After an eternal pause his mind returned from its heavenly bliss, eventually managing to process this information.

"Ehhh...Tommy. Sorry..eh."

"Hi Tommy Sorry, pleased to meet you."

"Eh no, sorry, it, eh, it's not...you know," he spluttered.

"I know, I'm just kidding," she laughed. "Just stop saying sorry."

"Sor...Ok. Yeah, good idea," he sighed, pausing to let his brain and nerves settle. "I like your hat." Just then, the door opened and a black clad figure swept into the room. As he paused for a moment to remove his black felt fedora hat, Tommy noticed the two up front beaming silently in tacit approval as they too removed their headgear.

"People, people, quiet people, ssh, ssh," requested the man in a high pitched, slightly camp voice, with more than a trace of a French accent.

"My name is...excuse me please, people, people, excuse me."

As the chattering died down he continued.

"Thank you people, now was that so difficult, eh?" he purred.

"My name is Mr Sylvain and I shall be your lecturer, mentor and guide on our journey together."

Mr Sylvain was a short slim man, mid-forties Tommy reckoned, with long black hair streaked with grey. Small round specs perched on his large Romanesque nose. Tommy and Katie shared a smile, leaned back and listened as Mr Sylvain outlined the course contents, what he expected of them, how they were in his hands and truly blessed to be there. He had been a respected documentary maker in France, winning awards for his films on the history of French cinema and a biography of singer Serge Gainsbourg. His two-man fan club gazed open mouthed, first at him, then each other, than back to their idol with barely contained, almost girlish glee. Suddenly, in the midst of Mr Sylvain's monologue, Tommy felt his head turn to Katie and say "Would you like to go for a drink later?" A jolt of panic shot through him as he realized what he'd done.

"That'd be nice, thanks."

Tommy waited for the panic to overpower him, but instead he was surprised to find himself feeling more at peace than he had in a long time. He turned back to the front trying not to grin, but failing.

CHAPTER 29

The next morning at Avon Park began as usual; with helping those who needed it get washed and dressed ready for the day. Most were reasonably mobile, but a couple of the old gents needed a hand. Old Sam Black, in particular was none too steady on his one remaining leg. His circulation was shot after decades of smoking Capstan full strength. Filter tips were for pansies, according to Sam. Eventually, his legs began to turn the colour of his lungs. One had to be amputated; the other was a dead man hopping. The artificial limb had fascinated Stevie at first. The detail of the foot, toes, even the texture made it incredibly life like. But then it seemed a bit of a waste of money. Who would see it? It's not as if he'd be walking along the Copacabana in his Speedos any time soon. Still, maybe the blue rinse brigade would be less creeped out if he got lucky. Leg and trousers on, Stevie helped him up, leading him towards the bathroom, but no further. Sam had told him in no uncertain terms what he thought of young boys who went to the bathroom with old men!

After seeing to another couple of old characters, he headed to the kitchen. Normally this was Senga's lair, but as she was off sick (fell off her broomstick, no doubt) and Rosie, a nurse Stevie had grown friendly with, would be late in from a dental appointment, this left Stevie in charge of breakfast. Having looked through the contents of the cupboards and fridge, then factored in his level of competence, Stevie decided that fried foods, eggs of any description and toast were out, which left a corn flake and muesli combo drenched in refreshing semi-skimmed. Throw in the customer's choice of teas, jammy dodger or custard cream, and there you had it. Breakfast a la Stevie. As people started to appear, he went to work. Rather than have a load of bowls ready, he'd decided to make each breakfast fresh. Nothing worse than soggy cornflakes.

"Morning ladies," he chirped to his first two customers, putting the bowls down.

"What'll it be, PG tips or Earl Grey?"

"Fried eggs," replied Muriel Grey stroppily.

"And sausages," chipped in Ethel Campbell.

"Yes, and sausages and bacon. And where's the toast?"

"We always have toast."

"This is much better for you. You don't want all that grease swishing about your arteries, eh? Not at your age," Stevie replied hopefully.

"I don't want this muck; I want sausages," retorted Muriel.

"And fried eggs and toast, we always have toast."

"Well I want a Ferrari, but that's not happening either."

The old ladies looked aghast.

"Look, ladies, ladies. I'll level with you..." Stevie's smile hiding the machinations beneath. "It was a dog."

"A dog," gasped Ethel. "I love dogs, used to have three. Great Danes. Beautiful."

"Oh, it wasn't the dog's fault Ethel, the fault was all mine. I...heard a dog outside and opened the door and there it was, a lovely Great Dane, looking for something to eat so I gave it a sausage, just the one mind, as I know how much you ladies like your sausages. But then...the phone rang, I went to answer it. When I came back the whole lot was gone, sausages, ham, eggs, everything."

"What about the bread, did it eat all the bread too?" sniffed Muriel tetchily.

"The bread?"

"Yes, for toast, we always have toast"

"Chewed beyond salvation I'm afraid."

"I suppose we can have a change for one day," said Ethel. "Poor dog, it must have been starving."

"Yes, it must have been. Poor thing."

"My arse," muttered Muriel under her breath. "We'll both have Earl Grey, assuming the dog didn't eat all the tea bags too."

"Two Earl Greys it is, and because you've been so understanding, you can have a jammy dodger and a custard cream."

"And me on a diet, too."

Stevie hated Muriel Grey.

A hundred lies later, thirty six sets of false teeth were grinding their way through bowls of muesli, or as one lady had so eloquently put it, "something you'd pick out of your arse if the

178

prunes hadn't worked". At 9.30am Stevie began collecting the dishes, pleasantly surprised that most were empty, ignoring the withering looks as he went, confident that the old dears would forgive him soon enough.

On a normal day after breakfast the residents would ...well... do pretty much nothing at all until lunch time. Maybe watch TV in the lounge, have a nap. After lunch, entertainment of some description was put on, usually provided by well-meaning volunteers. Today, however, Tommy was in charge and today would not be a normal day. By 10.30, most of the residents were in the main lounge. Only a couple had ambled gloomily back to bed, their continental breakfast left untouched. Such things were seen as further evidence of European interference in British traditions, and as such demanded at least a silent protest. Today's entertainment was Tom Park and his CD collection. Not exactly the cream of the Vegas strip, but it got a few toes tapping and a couple of the old dears up for a dance. Stevie smiled knowingly as the room grew louder with chat and laughter, jokes and gossip passing back and forth.

"Would you like some music on?" Stevie enquired.

"Yes, sonny, thank you very much," replied a now smiling Muriel.

"Ok Tom, you're on. I've set up some lights round the room, and a few behind you. I'll just shut over the curtains and turn them on, give the place a bit of atmosphere."

"Yes, I had noticed. All very showbiz, eh? Super."

As the coloured lights transformed the room, Tom took out the CDs he had prepared in advance and put the first one on. The sound of Glen Miller filled the air and the massed greys and blues filled the floor, turning back the years as the old ballroom memories came back. Feet that had stumbled were now gliding; dead eyes now glistened with life. Stevie watched as the shackles of age were abandoned, smiling as steps grew bolder, the moves more passionate, waiting until, after half an hour or so, he sensed a restlessness in the air and decided it was time.

"Ok Tom thanks very much mate."

"What do you mean, I've got lo-"

"All very good I'm sure, but I think they need something with a bit more oomf, so out the way, eh? Good man." Stevie turned to the room. "I think you want something a bit more lively eh?!"

"Yes!" They yelled back, momentarily startling Stevie with their enthusiasm.

As 'Rock Around the Clock' kicked things off, waltzes turned to jives, to the twist, through Buddy Holly, Elvis, Chubby Checker. The dancers showed no signs of waning as cardigans and shawls were discarded and time flew, Stevie taking them on his musical journey through the years, 60's, 70's, 80's, 90's... Up and up, Stevie built the energy. Higher and higher until...

"What the!-" exclaimed Rosie as she opened the lounge door, before jumping back to dodge the Zimmer frame hurtling past her head.

"Firestarter! Firestarter!" Roared the crowd in unison, bouncing up and down as the Prodigy anthem faded.

"I've already played it three times!" yelled Stevie, laughing.

"Firestarter! Firestarter!" they demanded, cheering as the intro began, and the strobe lights were activated once more.

Rosie stared in disbelief as blue rinse techno was born before her eyes. Rendered inert, she watched wide-eyed as thirty pensioners copied Stevie's imitation of the Prodigy front man's manic performance, frantically slapping their heads in unison to extinguish the imaginary flames. Snapping out of her trance, she filled her lungs. "Stevie!" she roared, "Stevie!" Finally she marched past the oblivious crowd, pulling the plug out of the wall. "What's going on?!" she screamed at the suddenly impotent DJ.

"Firestarter! Firestarter!" roared the frenzied mob.

"Firestarter, fuck all!" Rosie roared back. "Sit down the lot of you! Now!"

Lions turned back into lambs as they made their way slowly back to their seats. Stevie watched the life drain from them, as all their old aches and pains crept back, along with some new ones.

"What did you do that for?!" asked Stevie angrily

"Excuse me?"

"That was the first fun they've had for years, or at least since they've been in this dump!"

"How dare you!"

"I thought you were on their side, but you're just the same as the rest of them, just keep them quiet and have a nice easy shift."

"I take good care of them!" Replied Rosie, stung by the criticism.

"Care? Care? What about fun? Stevie and his special breakfast have given them more fun in one morning than they've had in all the time they've-"

"What did you say?" interrupted Rosie.

"Eh?"

"What do you mean, special breakfast?" She asked icily.

Stevie had been stunned by Rosie's reaction. He'd always seen them as kindred spirits, willing to go the extra mile. He'd expected Rosie to be thrilled that he'd given them a bit of life back, even unofficially. A nod and wink of approval. Them against the machine. But the piercing look in Rosie's eye's stopped him in his tracks as he tried to process the situation. He'd obviously misjudged things. He wasn't sure how, but that had to wait. She was now the enemy. He played for time.

"What do you mean, what do I mean?" He asked with practiced innocence.

"You said special breakfast."

"I said what?"

"Special fucking breakfast. What special breakfast? What have you done Stevie?"

"I've done nothing."

"What have you given them?"

Stevie knew he had run out of time.

"Muesli! I gave them muesli ok, instead of all that fried shit you give them. What are you trying to do, finish them off? Their cholesterol levels must be higher than a hard on in the Himalayas."

"Eh?"

"Just... really high ok, anyway, is it any wonder some of them can hardly move, having to digest a couple of pounds of lard first thing in the morning, I mean..."

Stevie's plan to deflect Rosie's suspicions by talking her into submission was abruptly cut short.

"Help! Help! It's Ethel, she's collapsed, help quick!" came a frantic voice.

Stevie stammered under Rosie's withering glare.

"So help me Stevie, if you've-"

"I didn't do anything."

As Rosie ran to investigate, Stevie's brain shut down. He watched as the dreamlike silent movie madness played out around him as it had once before. Arms waving, eyes pleading, lips moving, help out of reach. He watched as hope and Ethel were lost, knowing only one thing. He knew he had to leave. This time he walked home.

CHAPTER 30

Stevie paced up and down his bedroom his mind racing, round and round in a synaptic formula one. Maybe she'd just fainted? Maybe the E had nothing to do with it? Even if it had, would they know? But they'd do fucking tests wouldn't they, suspicious death and all that. Of course they'd find out and then what? He could explain. Yes, explain. Sorry your honour, old Ethel was looking a bit fed up so I slipped her some class A, or are they class B? Anyway, doesn't matter, illegal stimulants, into her ninety one year old body so she could make like Keith Flint...Keith Flint...singer from the Prodigy your honour...as in fi...Anyway, doesn't matter your honour, just some nutter, but she went for it old Ethel did, God bless her...Yes I'm sure He will too...but she had a great time...eh?...no your honour, not anymore...but she went out with a bang...better to burn out than fade away eh...Neil Young your honour...Hey, hey, my, my, from rust never sleeps, anyway...I know she's dead...No, maybe I didn't have the right but...She was dying anyway, slowly, withering a bit more every day...No, I'm not family...Yeah right...hang by the neck until I'm dead, yeah right, fuck you, your fucking ladyboyship, sitting up there like a big medieval tranny in your wig and your big posh frock!! "Aaaaaahhhh!" he wailed, slapping his face. "Snap fucking out it. Get your brain under control!" He sat down hard on the bed. "She might be dead, she might not be, but I can't take the chance. Let's fuck off for a few days, see how it pans out. If it turns out to be nothing, then back home it is. If she's pegged it...run." He grabbed his beat-up old canvas hold all from the cupboard, paused and looked around, but only for a moment. He knew he had to travel light and he knew he didn't have much time. He quickly ransacked his wardrobe and drawers. Pants, socks, jeans, tee shirts, a favourite green and yellow striped shirt, a few other odds and sods. Money. He'd need money. He quickly pulled up the floorboard and threw the bag of Es in. As good as.

"You got me into this mess; you can help get me out. If it turns out to be nothing, no harm done. If not, fuck Weasel." He was momentarily startled by a strange noise, it took him a moment to recognise as his ring tone. He sat frozen, just staring at the phone, uncertain what to do. But it could all be cleared up in a second, no need for any of this nonsense.

"Hello," he said in a soft, quivering voice.

"Stevie?" came a voice he recognised as Rosie.

"Yeah?"

"Stevie, where are you?"

"Eh nowhere, just...out."

"Stevie."

"Yeah?"

"You need to come back into work."

"Eh I don't feel very well. I'll be in tomorrow."

"You need to come in right away Stevie." her voice more forceful.

Stevie paused before asking. "How's Ethel?" he gulped, barely able to say the words.

"She's dead Stevie, the police are here. You need to come in, Stevie."

Stevie paused then hung up. His mind and path were now clear. He grabbed his bag and ran into the Kitchen. There he found a pen and piece of paper. On it he wrote the word: 'Sorry' and was gone.

CHAPTER 31

The Loft was located about 10 minutes from the university. Its name came from its location, atop a four storey Victorian building. A modest sized bar, it was set out as an array of booths, allowing a degree of privacy for illicit activities. The owners had taken a relaxed view on dope smoking over the years which had made it popular with students so inclined, though the smoking ban had put paid to that. The students, however, had remained loyal; finding no shortage of activities in which to indulge in the shadows. The décor was mock Cuban on crimson walls, with pictures of Castro, Guevara and heavenly Havana everywhere. Even in the toilets there was no escaping the omniscient gaze of El Presidente.

It was under this gaze that Tommy nervously availed himself of the facilities for the second time in fifteen minutes as he anxiously awaited Katie's arrival. Could he go through with it, or should he slip out before she arrived? As he washed his hands, the Clash's 'Should I Stay or Should I Go' began playing softly on the sound system, adding to the debate.

"Go," he whispered to himself. He quickly dried his hands and walked even quicker to the door, pausing for a second. Mind made up, he opened the door and exited, straight into Katie on her way to the ladies.

"Hi," she said, startled for a moment. "Back in a minute, can you get me an orange juice?"

"Eh, yeah, sure," he answered, regaining some composure. As he walked to the bar, one dilemma taken out his hands, he found himself in another. Should he order himself a beer or a soft drink? Maybe she didn't like drinkers? Maybe she was driving? Maybe she was a recovering alcoholic, who'd be straight on the phone to her AA sponsor at the first whiff of a half shandy? Maybe it would be Sharon Perry all over again? But that was all conjecture. One thing he knew. His nerves were shot and he needed something to take the edge off, just not enough to talk shit. That much he had learned. As the bar wasn't busy he was served quickly, ordering an orange juice and a bottle of Becks. The girl behind the bar was tall, blonde and stunning in hipster jeans and a tight black blouse opened two buttons past decency. She smiled at Tommy as she handed him his change. He smiled back, eyes lingering on her rear as she walked to the other end of the bar.

"Looks like I got here just in time."

Tommy's eyes turned quickly to meet Katie's, mock innocence meeting mock indignation, a wry smirk giving the game away. Tommy felt the temperature rise in his face and imagined how ridiculous he looked.

"I'm only joking," she laughed. "Let's sit over here," she said, pointing to a booth in the far corner.

"Yeah, sure."

Katie sat down first, their table obscured from the rest of the bar. Tommy put the drinks down, hands slightly trembling before sitting opposite her.

"Sit over here," she said, patting the seat beside her. "I won't bite."

Tommy grinned sheepishly and made his way round the table, trying not to knock anything over.

"That's better. I don't even know your second name, except it's not sorry."

"Slater, what's yours?"

"Don't ask."

"Come on."

She paused for a moment, before finally relenting.

"Caruthers," she sighed, her head dropping theatrically.

"Nothing the matter with that. I thought you were going to say something like…" As Tommy struggled to think of a funny name, Katie mercifully intervened.

"It's bad enough, I hate it. It's so… secretarial."

"Take a memo Miss Caruthers," laughed Tommy.

"Exactly, I can't wait to get married and be rid of it. " Now it was Katie's turn to blush. "I don't mean… Don't worry, I'm not out husband hunting."

"So why did you decide to do media studies," he asked, becoming more at ease.

"My dad's a TV producer, so he kind of encouraged me into it."

"Really? What programmes?"

"Nothing glamorous. Mainly outside broadcast stuff for local news programs, but you're not stuck in an office all the time. Gets you out and about, without having to dig things up or chop things down."

"Sounds alright," he laughed.

"What about you?"

"Eh, I dunno really...I knew what I didn't want to do. I knew I didn't want to work in a factory doing the same thing day in, day out. Nothing against factory workers, I know a couple and they hate it, ditto working in an office, or the same office all the time, like a bank or company. Working out in the pissing rain didn't appeal too much either. I just kind of went on like that and well...doesn't leave much."

"Not a lot."

"And I wanted to do something creative," he blurted out, giving away more than he intended. She put her arm on his shoulder. "Me too. I love drawing, painting..."

"Yeah? What do you paint?"

"People, candid stuff, I sketch them when they don't know. I've started trying to do landscapes in watercolours. It's hard though. I'd like to try oils sometime but... maybe when I'm a bit better."

"I'd really love to see them."

She smiled. "Maybe later, it'd be good to get an opinion."

"Has no one else seen them?"

"Mum and Dad, but you know what they're like. They love everything you do don't they?"

A pang of melancholy shot through him, his head lowering.

"What's the matter?" she asked, concern lowering her voice.

"Nothing, it's..." He paused. Unsure what to say, or whether he could say anything at all.

She put her arm around him, pulling him gently towards her. "You can tell me," she whispered. And he knew he could. He told her everything. What had happened on that night. What had happened since, with Margo and what she'd done for him and Susie, Stevie and their ups and downs and finally Susie's disappearance. Katie just held him and listened, barely believing what she was hearing, but never interrupting. She sensed his pain, still raw, but there were no tears from Tommy. They had been shed on many a solitary night when Susie was asleep, between nightmares. He just wanted to talk to someone. Someone who wasn't emotionally involved whose feelings he didn't have to be sensitive to, who could ease his burden, not add to it. No, the tears came from Katie, unnoticed at first, but as he finished speaking he lifted his head and turned to her. "Ge$ez. I'm sorry. I didn't mean to upset you." He gently wiped her tears away with his thumb.

"That's just so sad. How do you get through something like that? I don't know if I could. I mean your parents, then Susie..."

"Susie will be back," he said firmly.

"Sorry, I didn't mean...I'm sure she will. She just needs a bit of time to get herself together. Try not to worry. God, listen to me. I'd be worried sick."

"I'm the one who should be apologising. Not exactly a fun night out, me laying all this on you."

"Hey," she said, a hand gently placed on each cheek. "I'm really glad you could talk to me."

"Do you want another drink?" He asked.

"Would you like to have one back at my flat?"

"Yeah, I would. You could show me your pictures."

"I'd like that."

CHAPTER 32

"Well, this is it," said Katie, switching on the hall light.

Tommy stepped in close behind, almost too close, faintly clipping her heel on the way in. "Oops, sorry."

"You can't be drunk already," she teased.

Tommy blushed. "No, just clumsy."

She took his hand and led him into the living room.

"Have a seat. What do you want to drink? Beer or wine?" She asked.

"Eh...wine...eh no, I'll stick to beer."

"You can have both if you like."

"Beer's fine."

As Katie went to get them both a drink, Tommy looked around. The room was sparsely furnished. A couple of two seater couches and a coffee table filled most of the floor space. Across the room, shelves filled with books, DVDs and CDs drew his attention. After a brief search, he put on Frank Sinatra. Some mood music from old blue eyes as 'Fly Me to the Moon' crooned from the speakers.

"Are you trying to seduce me?" yelled Katie from the kitchen.

He was busted. "I love Sinatra."

"Me too."

On the walls hung large prints of the Buddha and Christ of St John of the Cross, alongside some smaller landscapes. Wondering if they could be Katie's, he stood up and took a closer look.

"They're terrible, aren't they?"

Tommy was startled for a second. "No, they're really good. You painted them?"

"Yeah. It's ok, you don't need to pretend."

"I'm not. Have you got any more?"

"Are you sure. You don't -"

"I'd really like to see them. Honest."

A moment later Katie returned with a brown leather folder, handing it to Tommy now seated on the couch by the window. As he began looking through them, she sat beside him. The first half dozen or so were fairly nondescript landscapes, but then came a series of religious pieces. Portraits of Christ crucified and resurrected, Saints deep in prayer, Buddha, face radiating serenely, and others he recognised as Hindu. Tommy studied the pictures intently, oblivious to being studied with equal intensity as Katie tried to gauge his reaction.

"Wow."

"Wow as in good, or wow as in what a nutter?" she asked cautiously.

"Nutter? No, these are really good."

Katie looked, saw no lies and allowed herself a smile. "You don't think its weird painting all this religious stuff?"

"Don't be daft, they're beautiful, not just pictures. They ...I don't know....come off the page at you. You can sense what they're feeling from the expressions...the emotions. Listen to me, the art critic."

"Everyone has opinions, critics just get paid."

"So do you believe, you know...in God and that."

"Oh here it comes."

"No, I didn't mean... I'm just asking that's all. Just getting to know you."

Katie thought for a moment. "Yes. Yes I do. What exactly God is, I'm not sure. But I believe in some sort of higher power."

"Even today, with science explaining everything?"

"Everything?"

"Well, nearly everything."

"Just because we have a better understanding of how things work doesn't mean there's no creator. We know how a PC works. Well I don't, but people do. Does that mean no one created it? I don't think Bill Gates made all that money from his good looks."

"I suppose so. Do you go to church?" Tommy enquired gently.

"No, it's not for me. I'm more into spirituality than religion. Religions seem too rigid, judgemental. We're all different; we need to find a path that suits us. I don't think there's one true faith, and all the rest are heretics. I mean, most people's religion is determined by geography, where you happen to be born. If you're born in Italy, you're a Catholic, but then someone from another religion calls you a heretic or infidel, or whatever, just because you were born in Italy. Doesn't make any sense to me."

"I know what you mean. They're like gangs. Us against them. Look at Jews and Muslims. Both believe in the same God, but hate each other more than atheists!"

"Yeah, I know!"

"I've always thought that religion is like communism, a good idea on paper, putting the needs of others before yourself and all that, but people just can't carry it off. Some could, but most of us are too greedy, ambitious, selfish."

"Especially people in power," replied Katie.

"So we're all in the crapper!"

"Exactly!"

As they sat silent for a moment, Tommy's mood sobered as another question came to mind. The one that had been gnawing at him in the weeks and months since the accident. "If there's a God..." He paused.

"Go on."

"If there's a God, why is there so much suffering in the world? Why do bad things happen to good people?"

Seeing the obvious root of the question, Katie hesitated before answering, knowing how easy it would be to say the wrong thing. "I don't have all the answers, Tommy," she replied gently, before continuing. "But the only way it makes sense to me is this: Take compassion, charity, helping someone in need. Good things, but they can't exist without someone needing that help, without someone suffering. Forgiveness is another virtue, but it couldn't exist without something to forgive, without hate, without cruelty. Good can't exist without evil. It's the opposites that drive life, without them people would just ...I don't know, sit about, not care about anything."

"But why to good people?"

"Karma, maybe. Even good people do bad things. In a previous life, good people may not have been so good."

The look on Tommy's face reined her back. "The other side of it, the positive side, is that if you live a good life, but bad things happen, maybe it means your next life will be better. I know it may not be much comfort if you're sitting dying of cancer, but it at least gives you hope, gives you a future. I'd rather think of it that way than life sucks and then you die. Wouldn't you?" Katie wondered if she'd gone too far, said too much, but after an awkward moment, she noticed the faintest trace of a smile.

"Yeah, I suppose so."

"Let's lighten things up. Want to watch a film?"

"Good idea. What have you got?"

"Have a look, see what you fancy, I'm easy."

Tommy browsed the titles until suddenly his smile broadened."

"What is it?" She asked.

"'The Searchers'. My favourite film. Didn't expect that."

"A John Wayne chick flick, eh?"

"That'll be the day!" They responded in unison.

Tommy's dad had given him the DVD as a present one year. Character building he'd said by way of explanation.

"You put it on and I'll get some drinks." Katie returned with two glasses of wine. "No more beer I'm afraid. Wine ok?"

"Fine. I didn't think you drank?"

"It's ok, it's communion wine."

"Oh, right, okay."

"I'm kidding you idiot!" she gasped, shaking her head. "I drink sometimes if the mood takes me." They both sat back as the film began, Tommy's arm draped gently on her shoulder.

"Do you believe that if you pray for something you get it?" asked Tommy.

"Yes...but not on a first date."

Tommy grinned, but his prayers lay elsewhere.

CHAPTER 33

Tommy awoke and immediately winced with pain, his neck lying at an angle last seen in the exorcist. "Ah, fuck," he groaned.

"Language," came a voice from the kitchen.

"Sorry," replied Tommy, slowly stretching past the confines of the two-seater settee, which had been his bed for the night.

"No need to ask how you slept."

"I'm ok, fine," came the unconvincing reply.

"Liar. You must think I'm a right old maid."

"No, I wasn't expecting...you know."

Katie relaxed, smiling. "What do you want for breakfast?"

"I'm fine."

"Sylvain on an empty stomach?"

"Good point. What kind of cereal have you got?"

"I'm having a fry up"

"Do we have time?"

"We do, we do."

"Then fry me to the moon."

Breakfast over, they collected their things and headed out. Just as Tommy was about to turn the handle, Katie stopped him and pulled him towards her, kissing him passionately. Tommy, startled at first, soon responded in kind, until responsibility splashed water on the flames.

"We're going to be late."

"You started it," laughed Tommy, turning his attention back to the door handle.

"I'm not an old maid, you know?"

"I noticed."

Katie smirked, satisfied that her reputation had been at least tarnished. "We are going to be late though. We'd better run."

Tommy took her hand and they ran, oblivious to wind and rain, dodging between traffic and pedestrians, raising their hands over startled passers-by, unwilling to break the bond, as they ran upstairs, past notice boards telling them nothing they wanted to know, through seemingly endless door after door after door, before collapsing in their seats beaming, fingers still intertwined with barely seconds to spare before the entrance of the Great Sylvain.

At the end of the day, they exited the way they had entered, albeit at a slower pace. Reaching the pavement, they stopped and turned towards each other.

"Do you want to come back to mine for dinner?" asked Katie.

"I'd love to, but I'd better be getting back home, keep an eye on things, just in case, you know." Sensing her disappointment, he hugged her for a moment. "I'll see you tomorrow. If you like we could go to the pictures on Friday."

"Okay," she replied, mood restored. "Have a think about what you want to see and we can talk tomorrow."

"Ok, speak to you later." He kissed her and headed off to the train station, turning

periodically to wave until she was out of sight...
And she was just that.

The journey home was a far more relaxed affair
than that of the previous day. Anxiety was
replaced by the fuzzy bliss of love's awakening,
as changing faces, stations and scenery passed
unnoticed. As he thought about how he was
feeling, he thought of a line from the film 'Jerry
McGuire' that Stevie and he had mocked
mercilessly as cinema's cheesiest moment, but
suddenly "you complete me" seemed as
profound an evaluation of his feelings at that
moment as he could come up with. He smiled
and thanked God Stevie wasn't there to witness
his betrayal. Then, just in time, he regained
sufficient awareness to recognise his stop.

As Tommy turned onto his street he was
confronted by flashing lights which, he soon
realised, were outside his house. His heart and
feet stopped. Suddenly, he was transported back
to an earlier night of flashing lights, knocked
doors, bad news and despair. Then he
remembered his prayer.

"Susie," he whispered, barely daring to hope
that maybe prayers were answered, that dreams
came true. Or was this another nightmare?
Before he knew it he was running, running as
fast as he could. He had to find out. Whichever it
was, he had to know. Adrenaline flooded his
system as he reached the door, almost knocking
over the exiting policemen.

"What is it? What's happened? Is it Susie? Have you found Susie? Is she ok? Tell me?!"

"Calm down son, calm down."

"But what's happened to Susie?"

"And who's Susie?" asked the burly officer softly, trying to calm the madman before him. The question brought a mixture of emotions as he realised she was neither found nor turned up dead. As Tommy tried to compose himself, Margo's voice came from behind the police officer, almost hysterical.

"It's Stevie, Son, they're trying to say he killed an auld woman, but I know he wouldnae dae that. He's a good boy, you know that, tell him Tommy, tell him Stevie wouldnae hurt a soul."

As Tommy's mind was sent spinning by Margo's revelation, the policeman spoke.

"Now madam, no one's saying he killed anyone. We just wish to speak to him regarding a suspicious death, that's all. So, like I say, if you know where he is or if he gets in touch, it really is in his interest to speak to us."

"I'll never betray my son. You lot have just got it in for him. He's a good boy."

"I'd remind you that harbouring a fugitive or being an accessory to murder are very serious offences."

"Murder?!" Exclaimed Tommy, struggling to process this latest drama.

"Now, let's not jump to conclusions. He's not been accused of-"

"But you said-"

"I was just saying...Look, just get him to contact us, ok?"

The policeman and his silent colleague got into the car, leaving a tear stained Margo and stunned Tommy in their wake.

"Let's go inside," said Tommy, taking her by the arm, guiding her into the house and sitting her down. "Look Margo, I know Stevie. I know he wouldn't hurt an old woman. It's just a mistake, that's all. No doubt about it, so relax. It'll get sorted out, don't worry. Ok? Nothing to worry about."

"Ok Tommy, ok, you're right, it's all just a mistake, just a mistake."

"What happened to her anyway?" asked Tommy.

"They say Stevie gave some old woman drugs and she died."

Tommy feared the worst.

CHAPTER 34

"This is your room. Remember. No alcohol, no drugs, no smoking, no fighting, or you're out. Understood?"

Stevie turned towards the greasy haired, broken spectacled, Napoleon complexed, streak of piss before him and wanted to punch him in the face. He stared at him for a moment, causing his host some unease, plugged in the earphones of his iPod, turned, entered the room and closed the door behind him. Lost for a moment in Lou Reed's 'Perfect Day', a hint of a grin broke through as Lou forlornly remarked.

"I wish I was someone else, someone good."

The irony of hearing it on an iPod he had stolen but two hours earlier hadn't escaped him either. "Oh, it's such a perfect day. It's not much, but it'll do," he sang softly, surveying his new surroundings. He'd expected worse. He'd expected filth, infestation and the stink of the devil, but it was reasonably clean and tidy. The furniture was beat-up, probably third hand, but for a low rent bolthole it would do fine. He began transferring what belongings he'd taken into the creaky wooden drawers, which led to the first dilemma. What to do with ten grand's worth of ecstasy? He sat for a moment considering his options, finally concluding he had three.
He could:

A) Hide it in a room with fewer hiding places than a butt-plugged politician in a gimp mask, surrounded by...well, people like Stevie.
B) Dig a hole and bury it, hoping no one would notice a youth walking the streets with a bag and a large shovel, looking for somewhere to dig.
C) Hide it in plain sight.

Thirty minutes later, Stevie was out on the street, the proud owner of a fluorescent yellow rucksack with enough narcotics to make the population of a small industrial town believe life was worth living. However, until he figured out how to turn them into cash, he had to find another way to get some money, especially as being a fugitive from the law ruled out any assistance from the state. It would take more than a fake beard or a comedy moustache to wangle that. His concentration was abruptly broken by a loud yell from the right.

"Want to buy a Big Issue sir, only one left." He was suddenly reminded of an old Monty Python sketch.

"Penny for an ex-leper," asked Michael Palin, energetically and healthily, bobbing up and down inside Stevie's mind.

"What do you mean an ex-leper?" he replied to the invisible python.

"Eh?" asked the baffled vendor.

"Nothing mate, nothing. Afraid I'm homeless too. Well, I'm in a hostel."

"Oh. Sorry, man," the vendor replied, deflated.

As Stevie stepped away, a thought occurred to him. "So, how do you go about selling the Big Issue?"

The young lad hesitated for a moment, sensing competition. However since it was a question to which he obviously knew the answer, and wishing to avoid confrontation, he spilled the beans. Stevie marched off in the direction given, happy that he now had a plan. Ten minutes later, however, he had a much better one.

CHAPTER 35

Tommy had spent most of the night trying to calm Margo, reassuring her of Stevie's innocence, that his phone was probably out of charge, that it was just a misunderstanding and he'd be back soon. All the while in his own mind, the cycle of condemnation, a conviction and sentence played over and over. He fought to hide any trace of doubt from Margo as he tried to convince her to get some sleep, assuring her it would be alright in the morning, before resorting to cider and a Night Nurse chaser.

She had still been asleep when he'd left that morning. He'd thought about staying with her, but couldn't face it. He had to get out. He also thought about giving his class a miss, the sparkle of media studies dulled by the shit storm currently engulfing him. And do what? It was raining outside, so the choice was be miserable and dry or be miserable and wet.

"Hi."

Tommy had been wallowing so deep he hadn't noticed Katie sitting beside him. He turned and smiled, wishing he had taken the wet option, in no mood for conversation.

"Hi," he replied wanly.

As the class began, Katie began scribbling down notes, but Tommy's eyes never left his desk. His mind felt heavy, sluggish, detached from its surroundings. Spent.

"What's the matter?" asked Katie, with a concerned whisper.

Tommy sighed, pausing for a moment. "I'll tell you later."

He had thought about telling her it was nothing; everything was fine, the usual lies, but maybe it was time to find out if there was something more here, before giving up completely. Between classes, further enquiries were met with further postponement, more silence, until they sat down at lunchtime.

"So are you going to tell me what the matter is, or are you just going to keep being melodramatic, and giving me the silent treatment?" Katie asked indignantly.

"My best mate's killed an old woman and legged it, and I've been up all night with his hysterical mum telling her it was all a mistake. Dramatic enough?"

Katie sat, mouth agape, trying to grasp what she'd been told.

"Who's silent now?"

"What happened?"

"The police came round to Margo's last night and told her that they were looking for Stevie. An old woman had died at the home where Stevie worked. They were treating it as suspicious, that it may have been drug related and that Stevie may have been involved."

"Why do they think that?"

"They didn't say."

"Do you think Stevie would do something like that?"

"Not deliberately, but with Stevie…things just happen. I've been trying to phone him, left messages, but he's not answering."

"Geez."

"What a fucking mess."

Katie took his hand. "How's his mum?"

"Sleeping or drunk."

"She must be worried sick."

"Yeah, she is. He's all she's got."

"What about Stevie's Dad?"

"Whoever that is."

"Don't you know?"

"Stevie doesn't know. She's never said. I don't know if she knows."

"So she's on her own. What a shame."

"Tell me about it," said Tommy wistfully.

Katie squeezed his hand tighter. "You're not on your own."

CHAPTER 36

Stevie stood for a moment and took in the view from his new workplace. The pitch he'd been given was not exactly a prime retail spot. Off the high street and with not a car park or train station in sight, it was not a place of easy captures. What little passing trade there was usually passed by at full speed. But for what Stevie had it mind it was almost perfect. It was 10 am and he was open for business. He noticed a middle-aged woman approach from his left and waited, getting ready, tension rising, now.

"Excuse me madam, can I interest you in a Big Issue?"

The only sign she gave of Stevie's presence was a sudden increase in speed as she whisked past, eyes firmly forward. It was a response he would have to get used to. Five minutes later, an old grey haired man entered Stevie's peripheral vision from the right, exiting stage left, leaving some non-specific advice on job hunting in between.

Four invisible men and two fuck offs later, Stevie had still to sell his first Big Issue.

"Fuck this," he muttered to himself.

Just then he noticed a couple of young guys walking towards him, probably heading towards the local college. It was time to move to plan B. They didn't look the fighting type so Stevie relaxed, keeping them under covert observation, waiting to see what happened, letting them make the first move. As they drew up, they looked at his magazines, then at him. That was a first, thought Stevie.

"We don't want a Big Issue," said the taller of the two.

"Well that's fine, cos I'm not fuckin selling any." They recoiled, pausing for a second, looking at each other, uncertain how to respond. Silently agreeing two against one weren't good enough odds, they turned away.

"I am however selling Es if you're interested?" They turned back, looked at Stevie, then again at each other. "How much?" enquired the shorter one tentatively.

"Ten quid each."

"That's a bit much; I only paid eight for the last one."

"If you want horse tranqs go to the vet. If you want Es come to me. I only sell good stuff."

"How do we know that?"

"Because I'll be here every day, that's how. If they're crap then you and your band of bitches at the college can come down with your hockey sticks and knitting needles and teach me a jolly good lesson. Or you can just fuck off. Your loss. You don't buy them, smart guys who actually have some money will. This stuff sells itself."

"We have money," stuttered the tall one indignantly.

"Good for you Stretch. Good for you. Plus, you get a free Big Issue."

"I told you we don't want a big issue."

"And how would that look?"

"Eh?"

"Like a fucking drug deal, you twat!"

"What are we going to do with it?"

"Read it, wipe yer arse with it, wrap it round yer cock and call it mummy, I don't give a fuck. What are you doing at college, cleaning the fuckin windows?"

"What do you think?" asked Stretch, ignoring the abuse.

"Why don't we try one each? Take them to Tom's tonight. Better get him one too."

Moments later, Stevie had thirty pounds in his pocket and was off and running.

"Remember, spread the word!" said the now smiling Stevie.

"Thought they sold themselves," fired back the short one.

"Ha fucking ha. Say hello to Snow White and yer six buddies for me."

For the rest of the day Stevie split the passers-by into two groups. Those inside his chosen demographic and those outside. Inside, or club 16-30 as he referred to them, was anyone inside that age group who didn't look like a policeman, librarian, Sunday School teacher, or in any other way too straight. Older, you had to look like Keith Richards. Anyone else was too risky. Especially kids. Also, no wannabee gangsters. Although enthusiastic consumers, they attracted the unwelcome attention of the police, or worse, their own regular dealers who had their own eleventh commandment. Thou shall have no other dealer but me. Or I'll chop yer fuckin legs off. If a straight approached, he would entertain himself by turning his back on them, in pre-emptive indifference. Anything more menacing would attract unwelcome attention. If Club 16-30, he would ask them if they wanted a Big Issue. Regardless of whether they answered in the positive, negative or blanked him, he would then follow up with an enquiry of a more pharmaceutical nature. More often than not, responses were positive. When it wasn't, Stevie tried to gauge the risk of being grassed, applying some subtle menace if considered necessary. As time went on his sense of who was right and who was wrong became more finely tuned. But he knew there was always risk. At the moment he was only keeping a handful on him at a time, the rest stayed in his rucksack, stashed under some rubble nearby. But it was still enough for an intent to supply charge.

A few hours later, a beggar he'd seen earlier down the high street came walking towards him.

"Alright mate? Had a good day?" asked the beggar.

"Yeah, pretty good, how about you?"

"Not bad. About fifteen quid. Enough to get out of it anyway," he laughed.

"Cool. I'm Stevie."

"Sid."

They shook hands and stood silently for a moment.

"You got a hostel?" asked Stevie.

"Na. There's an old derelict building near the river. That does me."

"Be a bit cold, eh?"

"Yeah, but I can do what I like. No fucker telling me not to drink or stop smoking. I've got a sleeping bag. A right good one, so it's not too bad. Well, most of the year. Stan here keeps me warm too."

"Yes, I'd noticed your dog. Hi Stan." Stevie bent over and rubbed his ears. Stan, who looked like an unfortunate cross between a Chihuahua and a Jack Russell, wagged his tail frantically. "Wish I had something for you to eat."

"Me too. He'll be starving. I'll need to see what I can find. I'll see you around. Take it easy."

"You too mate."

As the pair started on their way, Stevie turned and stopped them.

"Wait a minute. Look...I don't suppose you'd sell him.?"

"Sell him? Stan? No I couldn't man. We've been through too much together. He's my mate, you know?"

"Thirty quid and five E's?"

"He likes Whiskas, but he'll eat anything," replied Sid, handing over the lead.

CHAPTER 37

It didn't take long for word to spread and within a few weeks Stevie was doing good business, building up a solid group of regulars, mainly students, plus some friends of friends of friends. However with increasing numbers comes increasing risk and it was only a matter of time before his activities created a blip on the straight world's radar.

Head tilted downwards, Stevie's eyes tracked the figure across the street as it made its way with deliberate slowness to the end of the road. The man was early thirties, longish, curly brown hair. Wearing a dark blue anorak and jeans, there was nothing remarkable about the man, other than this was the third time he'd passed in the last hour. Stevie was also sure he'd seen him the previous day and turned his head slightly to continue his surveillance, watching intently as he approached a woman standing at the corner and engaged her in conversation. Sensing danger, he turned his attention to the other end of the road, and potential escape routes.

"Shit," he whispered.

At the other end of the street, on the same side as Stevie, stood another man, similar age, balding, moustache, lighter coloured anorak, also wearing jeans. As he turned back, the man and woman, who had now crossed the street, were walking slowly towards him. Guessing he had about thirty seconds, Stevie put his hands in his pockets and slowly sat down on the pavement beside Stan, watching the pair from the corner of his eye, seeing them smile, sensing victory. Twenty seconds.

"So you'll eat anything eh? Dinner time Stan," he whispered, transferring his stock from pocket to hand under the cover of his jacket. Stan stuck his nose under and wolfed them down in a split second. Sensing their disappearance, Tommy quickly and seamlessly moved his hand to the side of the dog's head, patting and stroking him with practised innocence.

"Big issue? Not many left," he asked the approaching couple.

"It's not the big issue we're looking for," replied the woman taking her warrant card from her coat pocket.

Stevie had decided some time ago that if a situation like this ever happened he would play innocent and keep his mouth shut. No smart arse remarks, no piss taking, and no hinting that he'd beaten them.

"Always happy to help the police in any way a humble street vendor can." Stevie winced inside. This wasn't going to be easy.

"We've heard you're selling more than the Big Issue," came the voice from his left.

"Empty you're pockets."

"On what grounds?"

"On the grounds that we're telling you to empty your fucking pockets."

"Get up, hands against the wall," demanded the woman.

Stevie did as instructed and the first man began his search, first pockets, then patting him down, before getting more intimate than Stevie thought decent or legal, struggling to keep the lid on the erection jokes bubbling away in his brain.

"Nothing."

"I'll have a look," replied the second man. The second, more forceful search was no more fruitful than the first. Stevie was about to demand a full cavity search by the remaining, rather pretty female officer, when the realisation that he may actually get away with it rode in to save the day.

"Look, I get abuse from people every single day. Some people just hate us. That's what this is. Let me guess, an anonymous tip off?"

The three officers looked at each other, said nothing and walked off up the road as fast as their humiliation would take them. Tommy's gaze followed them, every step, taking nothing for granted. Once they were out of sight he allowed himself a smile, but that was all. He had another matter to attend to. Looking down, Stan's tail seemed to be wagging faster than usual. Other than that he seemed ok, but Stevie knew he had to act quickly. Sitting back down, he removed a bottle from his coat pocket.

"Medicine time Stan and you're not going to like it." He held the open end of the bottle towards the dog, and as he opened his mouth, forced the neck of the bottle in and clamped his hand round the dog's snout, before tilting the bottle, decanting its contents into the helpless animal. Two seconds later the salt water and its illicit flotsam were retched onto the pavement.

"Good dog, Stan. You get them up, Son."
Stan turned to look up at his owner, feeling anything but a good dog.

"Sorry mate, I know how you feel. I learned that from an expert. Here, have one of these. Might freshen you up a bit, eh?" Stevie held out one of Stan's favourite mints, which was taken with uncharacteristic caution, as he fixed Stevie with a look of suspicion and a subliminal growl. However, half a packet later all traces of post-traumatic stress had been eliminated. Looking down at the soggy cargo, Stevie picked one up and dried it off. Although a little frayed around the edges, the tablets gave little indication of being partially digested. Satisfied, he salvaged the rest.

"Waste not want not, eh Stan? They'll never know." Stan was keeping silent on the matter. "Fuck it, let's call it a day and get you something to eat eh. Whiskas Stan?"

Stan's tail confirmed him as an eight out of ten cat.

"Let's roll!" he barked.

CHAPTER 38

Back at the hostel Stevie sneaked the dog into his room under his coat. Stan had learned a long time ago when to keep quiet and rarely barked indoors or around other people. Although animals weren't allowed on the premises, Stevie had come to a carrot and stick agreement with the hostel commandant. The stick was the knife Stevie had taken to carrying for protection, or so he told himself. In truth, its purpose had become more about intimidation and persuasion. As for the carrot, that was a few freebies dished out from time to time. Although clean and sober for five years, or so he'd said, it hadn't taken much encouragement for him to take the occasional holiday from reality, but as long as he kept his mouth shut, Stevie was happy.

Up in his room Stevie spooned half a can of Whiskas onto a plate and filled a bowl with water. "Tuck in Stan, you've earned it today." Stevie sat back and watched him. As he did he became aware of a strange feeling coming over him. It took some time before he recognised it as loneliness. Having cut himself off from his previous life, the only friend he had now was the little dog making a mess of the floor in front of him. The only one he could talk to...couldn't talk back. Everything that had happened in his life, all his memories had been cut adrift. There was no one in his life now who knew about that stuff, who could keep it alive. It was all gone. What did he have left? He couldn't go on as he was. Apart from the Es running out, he needed something, a purpose, a future, one that didn't just involve spreading shit through the world. Maybe make amends for some of his fuck-ups. Ease the guilt that had been gnawing away ever since that night, no matter how often he told himself it wasn't his fault. But for the moment looking after Stan would have to do.

"So what are we going to do tonight, Stan? Fancy a DVD? Lassie come home, eh? Let's see what's on first."

Stan's scarred little face seemed to light up as his tail drummed off the table leg. Stevie had bought himself a portable TV with built in DVD player. Risky, given the hostel was more or less a holding area for the local prison, but a risk worth taking given that the alternative was terminal boredom. No, a TV was a must have and if someone nicked it, well they wouldn't be far. He turned it on to be met with the usual snow and hiss.

"Feck, here we go," he moaned, picking up the indoor aerial and searching for the hotspot, twisting and moving the aerial as if flying a model aeroplane. But tonight, all the aerobatics in the world weren't delivering a picture and he crashed the aerial into the bin defeated. "Fuck it! You stay here Stan; I'll go and get a DVD." Stevie patted the bed. "Up you get and if any cunt tries to nick anything, you bite them in the balls."

The streets were empty as Stevie stepped lightly across the pot-holed pavements of Barrhead road, with only the blues and his frosted breath for company. Up ahead was his destination, Planet Video, though why planet video when it only stocked DVDs...Anyway, here he hoped he'd find something to take his mind off the mess that was his life, or at least kill a few hours. He crossed over just before the streetlight, wary of visibility, of being laid bare for inspection, for judgement. As he approached, another seeker of distraction entered just in front of him. Stevie thought about abandoning the mission, but went to the other side of the shop and started looking through the titles. As he searched through row after row of films he'd never heard of, he started to think it might be porn night. At least with the adult section you only had to concern yourself with the first 10 minutes, but then that didn't help pass the desperate, dragging minutes, hours and days. Maybe a mixed assortment, a thriller (hopefully with an occasional thrill), crime drama (bang bang, motherfucker, bang bang) and 'Madam Spanky strikes again volume 1'. He had a look over to see who was on the till as it was slightly less embarrassing to hire porn if a guy was on, but tonight a rather sweet looking girl was seated behind the counter, looking every inch the Sunday school teacher.

Just as his mind's eye began stripping the lovely young miss, his attention was distracted by the man who had entered before him. He was thin, scrawny, maybe 30, long greasy hair and an obvious soap dodger of the highest order. He could smell him from the other side of the shop, the long coat that he wore unable to contain his putrid fragrance. For a speedy exit, Stevie quickly decided that tonight was wank night and made his way towards the counter, putting down his selection along with his membership card. Just before the big blush, Stinky pushed him aside and stepped up to the counter.

"Open up the till and put all the fucking money in this bag!!"

The girl froze, looking at the gun in his other hand.

"Fill the fucking bag."

"Better do as he says, love."

"Shut the fuck up, dickhead. I give the fucking orders."

"Course you do chief, I'm only saying. She's scared shitless. "

The girl had by now started crying and was still unable to move.

"Last warning you stupid bitch, open the fucking till!"

"Calm down, you'll get your money. You too sweetheart, calm down and-"

"You don't fucking tell her to calm down! I fucking tell her to calm down!"

"Well go on, then."

"Go on what?"

"Tell her to calm down."

"I don't want her to calm down, I want her to give me the fucking money and you to shut your big fucking yappy mouth, ya fucker."

"My, you have an almost musical way with our mother tongue."

Stinky's eyes narrowed and he turned the gun towards Stevie. "You're going to die you fucking asshole."

Stevie sighed. "Yes, sadly I am...but not tonight." He then brought the knife he had removed from his pocket up and across the wrist pointing the gun, which fell to the floor. Stinky yelped in painful surprise as the knife came back across his throat, turning yelp to gurgle in a fraction of a second. He forced both hands against the wound, trying in vain to stem the breached dam, looking in disbelief as blood sprayed between his fingers before falling to his knees as if in final prayer. Seconds later he collapsed on his side into unconsciousness and death. Stevie paused for a second to allow events to fully register, awaiting his thanks from the rescued maiden.

"You've killed him," she whispered.

"Indeed I have," he replied, his voice tinged with pride.

"Oh my God, what have you done?"

"Eh? Saved your life that's what I've done. I'm a fucking hero."

The girl started screaming and Stevie, heroically, punched her in the mouth, ruining her Sunday school smile forever and sending her careering into the "on hire" DVDs. He turned to the body on the floor. "Could you not have held the place up after I got my film, you cunt!" He turned and looked at the terrified woman.

"Don't know why I bother. Ah well, lucky dip it is," he said, grabbing a handful of discs. He then stepped over the body and made for the exit, before stopping and turning back. "Nearly." He whispered as the reached over to the counter and picked up his membership card, checked for CCTV and left.

On the way home Stevie once again kept out of sight, walking in the shadows, keeping his distance in the dimly lit streets and just as well to. He only realized how horrific he looked when he opened the door and saw Stan's face, just before he disappeared under the bed. Now in full light, he looked in the mirror above the sink, appearing exactly as he was, the star of a slasher movie. He stood silently for a moment just taking it in, turning his head to view the splatter patterns before calmly stripping off the blood soaked clothes and putting them in a plastic bag. Next he washed himself as best he could, figuring if he got most of it off clean clothes would cover the rest until he could have a shower. Soon the cops would be swarming about and Stevie's thoughts turned to flight, but realising that a sudden disappearance would just attract attention, he decided to stay put for now. But what about the knife? He loved it. A proper combat knife. Razor sharp. Weasel had given it to him "just in case", and he was loath to get rid of it and decided he'd hide it with his stash when the coast was clear. Once dressed, he went outside to check the stairs and floors for blood. Miraculously there were only a few spots, which he burned out with a lighter he had stolen from some flash businessman just for the hell of it. Scorch marks blended in with the hostels decor. Blood probably wouldn't have been noticed either, truth be told, but better to be safe. When he got back to his room, Stan was nowhere to be seen. "Stan? You there? Stan?" A small head appeared from under the bed and once satisfied the monster was gone the rest soon followed. "Did I give you a fright, wee man?" He asked as he picked him up, laughing as any remaining traces of evidence were thoroughly removed with a mixture of sandpaper and spit. "Easy Stan, I know where that's been," but he didn't care. "This doing good shit's not all its cracked up to be."

CHAPTER 39

Margo sat slumped in her chair, eyes fixed on the glass in her hand as she swished the vodka round and round, a hypnotic distraction from the panic-laden imaginings going round and round in her mind which a sea of alcohol had failed to fully submerge.

"I rang the bell but nobody answered," said the voice from behind her.

It fared no better. Its owner walked past and sat down in the chair opposite, looking gravely at Margo.

"How are you?"

Margo remained fixed on the glass.

"Any word on the boy?"

The glass stopped before being raised to her lips and emptied.

"That's not going to help Margo."

"Don't you fucking lecture me about drinking! You of all people? You're having a fucking laugh."

"Has he not phoned at all?"

The question met with more silence.

"He's a selfish little bastard."

"And who's fault's that eh?!" screamed Margo. "What the fuck are you doing here anyway? What do you care?"

"I care. Of course I bloody care!"

"Why? Feeling guilty all of a sudden?"

"I've nothing to feel guilty about."

"Nothing!? Not a bit of interest all these years and suddenly it's all concern."

"Whose fault's that!? I followed you down here didn't I, but you made it clear you didn't want me anywhere near."

"You didn't take much persuading did you?"

"I would have tried, did my best if-"

"Your best is nothing! You're a waste of space."

"You made that clear too, never miss a chance. It was your choice. It's always your choice."

"That's right and I chose you to get to fuck. It's got nothing to do with you."

"He's my son too."

"He's my son! Mine! You hear? He's all I've fucking got."

"At least you had him, been part of his life, not had to watch from a distance like a spectator, like a bloody stranger."

"I suppose it's all my fault, eh?"

"I'm not saying that, you did your best but boys need…"

"What? A dad? A man about the place? A role model? Is that what you think you are? What kind of fucking role model are you. Do you think he'd look up to you?"

"Maybe I wouldn't have ended up like this if-"

"So that's my fault too eh? I made you a-"

"I'm not saying that."

"Role model. Just watch me, Son, I'll show you how to be a drunken arsehole! Life in the gutter? I'm yer man, come on down. Aye right. We did just fine. I didn't need you. He doesn't need you. We got along just fine." Margo sobbed as she filled her glass.

"Us fighting's not going to help and neither's that. I know better than anyone."

"It'll do for now. Just go, eh? Leave me be."

"Let me know if you hear anything then... Please."

"Ok, ok. Just go."

Brushing a tear from his eye he got up and walked soberly to the door, his hand fleetingly squeezing her shoulder as he passed. Then, as he turned for one last silent look, Hughie closed the door behind him.

CHAPTER 40

"Hi."

Tommy smiled at Katie's voice on the phone. "Hi. How's things?"

"Good. Great actually. I've got something to show you. Can I come over?" asked Katie, voice crackling with excitement.

"Eh...I...eh..."

"You got something on?"

"Eh...no, but..."

"But what? Are you embarrassed to be seen with me?"

"You must be joking. If anything it's the other way round."

"Now who's being daft?"

"But...it's a bit nuts round here just now with one thing and another. Margo's not...you know...she's struggling a bit. I don't think she's ready for visitors"

"Oh, ok. Maybe..."

Just then, another familiar voice interrupted.

"My arse! I'm fine. Don't you listen to him, dear. You come 'round right now. I've been dying to meet you. I was starting to think he'd made you up."

"Margo, get off the phone, this is a private call."

"You can talk about your privates later Tommy, but me and Katie will have a cup of tea and a chat first, or dinner. Have you eaten, dear?"

"I've just had dinner thanks but a cup of tea would be nice. If I leave now I'll just make the

6.30 train, if you could meet me at the station, Tommy?"

"Ok," came the reply, echoing from two different sources before hanging up.

Tommy walked down the stairs, each step more reluctant than the last, until just giving up.

"Okay," he muttered under his breath. "If you want warts and all, you got it."

And they didn't come much wartier than Margo.

Tommy's face beamed as Katie stepped off the train. When he was with her, light seemed to shine through even the darkest clouds. They hugged, prolonging it, as if to gather strength from each other before making for home, uniting to face, well, that was the question. For Tommy it was simple, he didn't want Margo screwing things up with the first girlfriend he'd had, not counting Sharon, which would be stretching things a bit. Yes, Margo had been good to him, actually a hell of a lot more than that, but wasn't he still entitled to a life of his own? As for Katie, all she had to go on were the picture Tommy had painted of Margo, worthy of Van Gogh in mid Absinthe binge. But she also sensed her goodness and the love Tommy obviously had for her.

"Look, just so you know, she's not exactly what you'd call...refined. She-"

"Do you think I'm a snob, Tommy?"

"No," replied Tommy startled by her tone. "But you're from a more...classy background. Good jobs, money, more up market."

"What a snob you are!" exclaimed Katie, bemused by Tommy's rambling.

"No I'm not. It's just, Margo is..."

"She took you in, looked after you and Susie. That tells me she's pretty fucking great, in my book, anyway."

Tommy flinched at the first swear word he'd heard from those angelic lips.

"It's just, she's a bit over the top sometimes. I'm used to her but some people can be overwhelmed."

"Well, I'm not some people."

"I just don't want you to be scared off"

"I'll try and be brave for you," she laughed. "Relax, Tommy; I'm not here to judge anybody."

"Ok, ok, let's just see what happens."

As they reached Tommy's, he breathed deeply, reaching slowly for the door handle before finding it suddenly torn from his grasp. Tommy was stunned by what he saw. The familiar pantomime dame had been abducted. Her obviously fake replacement, dressed in pastel greys and blues, seemed as sober as her attire, verified by a discreet sniff of her breath. Minty fresh, with no vodka undertones.

"Margo? You look...."

"Oh be quiet Tommy, let the girl get in and sat down. The kettle's just boiled, what do you take Katie, dear? Milk, sugar, lemon?"

"Lemon?" sniggered Tommy.

"Milk, no sugar, please Margo."

"Us girls, eh? Always watching our figures, not that you need to, lovely little thing that you are. I'll just be a minute."

As they sat silently, facing each other, Katie raised her eyebrows quizzically. Tommy shrugged his shoulders in silent reply.

"You're awful quiet through there!" shouted Margo from the kitchen.

"Just waiting for you, Margo!" replied Katie.

A moment later, Margo re-entered, a tray with 3 cups, saucers, and a plate of biscuits balanced in her left hand at an alarmingly steep angle. Tommy tensed, fearing the worst, watching in slow motion as they came into land.

"There we go, never spilled a drop, as the actress said to the bishop. Your father's not a bishop, is he?" She chuckled.

"No, no he isn't, just a priest. But one day, God willing."

Margo paled. "Shit. I mean….No offence dear, just a wee joke."

"I'm only kidding, Margo."

Margo deflated into her chair, as relief filled her face. "Oh Jesus, are you trying to kill me, dear?"

"Sorry, Margo," giggled Katie.

"I can't tell you how good it is to see Tommy with a girlfriend. I thought I was going to have to knit him one."

Tommy's face reddened.

"Really? I thought he was a bit of a charmer, a real ladies man."

"Tommy? Oh no. Shy. Too quiet for his own good. But handsome eh?"

"Oh, he's not bad."

Tommy, by now scarlet, could stand no more. "I'm sitting right here, you know."

"We're talking about you, not to you dear."

"Well talk about something else."

"What about you Katie? Tell me about yourself, since Tommy's told me absolutely nothing."

"She didn't come here to be interrogated," countered Tommy defensively.

"It's ok, I don't mind."

Tommy looked over to see Margo sticking her tongue out at him. Outflanked and outnumbered, he sat back in surrender and left the women to it. Two life stories were unfurled and exchanged, their narrative fuelled along the way by "something a bit stronger." Tommy watched as his Margo returned, more and more visible behind the thinning disguise, makeup smudged, words slurred, and yet the more she did the greater gal pals her and Katie became, as she tried to match her drink for drink, growing more intoxicated with every revelation, every secret revealed, every juicy bit of gossip. As Tommy sat back and listened, sipping from his own well stocked glass, it seemed to him that this was what made the world go round. Not money, not power, unfortunately not love either. Gossip. Whether it's who Mrs X down the road is having an affair with, Hello magazine and it's who's who of celebrity rehab, or the Six O'clock News letting you know who's getting blown to fuck today, it didn't matter. It was the civilised world's obsession. But why, he wondered? And why was only bad news interesting? Is that what we rely on to give a glimmer of hope, an ounce of self-esteem? The knowledge that someone somewhere has a shittier life than you. Ten minutes of celebrity whining would put a spring in anyone's step. But gossip and alcohol, now there's a cocktail. So he had another drink, and another, listening to the ladies while trying to formulate his own manifesto on life, before giving up, concluding instead that life is like trying to work your way through the Karma Sutra with a one legged virgin. Hard work, always teetering on the brink of disaster.

"You're awfully quiet, Tommy," came a voice from the other side.

"Eh, just enjoying the conversation."

"You didn't hear a word, did you? See, that's what he's like, away in a world of his own. Anyway you didn't come to listen to me gas all night; up you go to Tommy's room."

"Ok," replied Tommy, relieved and grateful.

And up they went without a word, both swaying as they climbed the stairs, holding tight to the handrail. Tommy closed the door behind them and they both sat on the bed, unsure what to do next. Suddenly Tommy noticed the black padded case Katie had kept beside her all night.

"What's that?" he enquired squinting.

"Oh, that's what I was talking about earlier. Dad gave me it to help with the course work. It's his old one."

"His old what?"

She opened the case and pulled out a video camera.

"Wow, sweet. Let's see it."

She handed it over to a child on Christmas morning. Eyes wide, fingers frantic, he pushed every button in turn. "What does it take?"

"Sorry?"

"What does it record on?"

"8mm tape. High resolution. It's quite old, but good quality. You can transfer to a computer then edit it. He gave me software for that too," she explained, as she set up the telescopic tripod.

"Cool."

"I've got lights too, for indoor stuff."

"Really? Brilliant. Let's set it all up."

"You put the camera on the tripod and I'll set the lights up."

Five minutes later they were on set, imaginations in overdrive, the movies they would make, jumping excitedly from project to project. But their innocent Hollywood daydreams were quickly dissolved.

"Aye, it's always the quiet ones right enough. I hope I'm not disturbing you. You should have said you were making a wee porno for yourselves. I'd have gone out, given you a wee bit of privacy."

Momentarily struck dumb, Katie was the first to reply. "No, no we're not-"

"It's nothing like that," interrupted Tommy, now brighter than the camera lights.

"It's ok, nothing the matter with a wee private sex tape, not these days, everyone's at it."

"But we..." Katie tried in vain to explain.

"Really, don't be embarrassed. I've done it too. Frankie Foster and Albert Clarke. Not together though, but-"

"Margo, we don't want to know!" interrupted Katie.

"Albert Clarke!? The butcher?" gasped Tommy, in disbelief.

"Believe me, he's more T bone than sausage, even if he's a bit on the chubby side," explained Margo.

"Chubby! He's like a walrus; he's even got the moustache. How did you even find it?"

"Like I said, more T b-"

"Enough, enough," pleaded Katie, fighting off the images developing in the devils darkroom. "Sorry dear, I'm holding you back. I'll away round to Albert's, you've got me in the mood now! I'll see you in the morning. Have fun, and remember to move the camera about, makes it seem like there's someone else in the room, makes it, you know, dirtier. Anyway, I'll be off." With that, she went, straight through every door between her and her prey, hornier than a rampant rhino on Viagra. The two young lovers left in her wake were struck speechless once again. Disorientated, Tommy recovered first.

"Albert Clarke. Geez."

"I need a drink," laughed Katie. "You want one?"

"A very large one."

Katie returned a minute later swigging a bottle of cheap red wine. "Think Margo must have taken the Vodka." She sat down heavily on the bed and offered the bottle to Tommy.

"I thought you didn't drink much?" he teased.

"So? Don't be a killjoy. Can't a girl have a good time?"

"Sure" he said, tipping the bottle back.

Katie put her hand on his leg, before leaning over and pushing her tongue into his ear. She then pointed at the camera and smiled, licking her lips as she did. "Film me."

"Eh? Are you sure?"

"I wanted the first time to be memorable, and what could be more memorable than filming it? Just keep it to us, though."

Tommy was behind the camera before Katie had finished speaking. He switched on the lights, focussed and pressed record. As she knelt on the bed with her back to him she turned her head, with a look of glassy-eyed seduction. He began to unzip his trousers, but-

"Not yet!" she commanded. With one hand on each side she slowly lifted her skirt, pausing as she saw the anticipation register on his face, raising it slowly, listening to his breathing grow heavier at the sight of the briefest of white panties.

Tommy started to come towards her.

"Not yet Alfred Hardcock, keep directing, I'll tell you when." Hooking her thumbs into the waistband she slowly, millimetre by millimetre, slipped them down. Tommy gasped at curves sublime, yearning to touch, before suddenly they were gone. Katie rolled over onto her back, knee's together, underwear dispensed with before carrying on where she'd left off, beginning the slow striptease again, each blouse button mocking him in turn before the satin garment was eased over her unblemished shoulders. As she reached behind to unfasten her matching bra, Tommy again had to be chastised, until finally her beckoning index finger found an obedient servant. As he knelt on the bed above her, she reached for the bottle, put it to her lips and drank, then ran her tongue around the rim before passing it to her impatient lover. Tommy drank, then looked at the bottle, and then looked at Katie.

"Don't even think about it."

Tommy put the bottle down, unsure of the next scene.

"Now it's your turn," she said, turning and winking to the camera.

Just then Tommy's phone beeped with an incoming text.

"Ignore it."

"It's Margo, might be important." He opened it hurriedly; impatient to get on with what was shaping up as the best night of his life. And wished he hadn't... picture proof.

Margo had got her threesome.

CHAPTER 41

The next morning Tommy awoke with a smile even hell's own hangover couldn't budge. He turned his head slowly to check it was all real, had actually happened, wasn't just a hazy wishful dream. But there she was. Smeared make up, mussed up hair, morning breathed and beautiful. Right then he knew he loved her. He lay still watching her breathe, a romantic cliché he now tenderly grasped. She turned unconsciously, now facing him, and he slowly moved over to kiss her softly, not wanting to wake her, failing. Her eyes opened uncertainly, her mind focusing, regaining consciousness, suddenly finding herself under siege from morning after memories, embarrassment, guilt, and shame. As she felt herself being overwhelmed, the eyes gazing into hers told her it was fine, that she could do or say anything and not be judged, not be ridiculed, just loved unconditionally. She kissed him back.

"I must stink."

"I'm not feeling too fresh either."

Then they made love.

Afterwards, they both showered and dressed, Katie borrowing a pair of Tommy's pants. It was either that or Margo's. They then made up the bed before sitting on it, listening to the Byrd's 'Sweetheart of the Rodeo'. Tommy had never been a country music fan, but the Gram Parsons incarnation of the previously psychedelic 60's pop band had convinced him of its merits, leading him to re-evaluate greats like Hank Williams and work forward, to see it as the white man's blues. Sure, old whitey had never had to work the plantations, wake to burning crosses or the fear of lynching, but tragedy, heartache, love found and lost, not forgetting death, these were all part of the human condition, blind to skin colour. They sat quietly for a while, but neither could remain blind to the elephant in the room.

"So....What about the tape?" enquired Katie tentatively.

"What about it?"

"I don't...I don't know...I'm not..."

"It was just fun wasn't it?"

"Yeah...but."

"You were great. God...Sexy as hell, honestly."

"You mean drunk."

"We were both a bit drunk, but not that bad."

"Still, I'm a bit embarrassed."

"Don't be. Don't ever be. I think you're...I love you, so don't ever be embarrassed with me."

"What did you say?"

"Don't be embarrassed."

"No what else?"

Tommy looked at her and smiled. "I said I love you. Now I'm embarrassed."

"Don't be, I love you too, but what if someone saw it?"

"They won't, I'd never do that."

"I believe you, but what if someone found it."

"I know a place. There's some floorboards in Stevie's room that lift up. He used to hide stuff."

"Stuff?"

"Yeah...drugs...you know...stuff."

"Even so, maybe Margo knows about it. I think we should erase it."

Tommy sat deflated, though not surprised. Katie had never struck him as the porn type. But then.

"Ok, why don't we watch it first."

"Great!" blurted Tommy, failing to disguise his enthusiasm. "Now?"

"No. There's no way we're watching it when Margo could walk in."

"She'd probably want a copy."

"I'm going to Mum and Dad's tonight, but we can watch it at mine tomorrow night if you want?"

"You need to ask? Don't watch it without me though."

"I wasn't going home right now; we could chill here for a while. I'm feeling a bit rough anyway. Tomorrow night we could go out for a bit, get something to eat, then back to mine, have a drink and...you know."

"Yeah. I know. Don't know about the drink though, I'm feeling a bit rough too," he said wearily, the hangover gaining traction.

"I don't know if I could watch it sober," countered Katie.

"Don't be shy."

"I can't help it."

"I'm shy too."

"Not that shy."

"You know I am. I might have been rubbish."

"I don't remember you being rubbish, but my memory is a bit hazy."

"Not exactly the ringing endorsement I was fishing for."

Katie laughed. "So, what was Stevie into then?"

"How'd you mean?" surprised at the sudden change of subject.

"Drugs."

"Em, ecstasy mainly...speed, hash"

"Did you ever try any?"

Tommy was unsure how to respond. If he said yes, did he sound like an exciting "bad boy" or just a sad junkie loser? If he said no, did he sound boring? What would she want to hear? He chose the truth. "Now and again I took the odd E with him, smoked the odd joint."

"Really?" replied Katie, sounding surprised. Before he could back pedal, Katie continued. "So, what's it like?"

"Ecstasy?"

"Yeah."

"Pretty ecstatic."

"No, really."

"I mean it. You just love everyone. Party central."

"Really?"

"Really, truly, straight up, up and away."

Katie pondered for a moment. "Did he leave any when he went?"

"Why?"

"Just...wondering."

"He had a big bag stashed away, hundreds, maybe even thousands."

"Really?"

"Don't start that again."

"Sorry...Wow."

"But he took it with him when he left."

"Oh, ok, just wondered."

"He did give me a couple the week before though."

"Re...sorry, did he eh?"

"Yeah."

Another period of silence followed, as they both sought to navigate the uncharted territory of new love.

"Do you think I'd like it?" she asked, with a naughty schoolgirl look.

"Look, I don't want to get you into drugs and stuff like that. I've seen some of the people Stevie dealt with. It can be a bit seedy."

"Are you a bit seedy then?"

"No, but..."

"But what?"

"I just didn't think you'd be into it, that's all."

"I'm not. I'm just curious. I mean, you've tried them, so they're not cut with poison or anything like that?"

"No, but they are illegal, you know."

"Alcohol's legal, tobacco's legal. How many people do they kill?"

"I know, I know, I just don't want to..."

"I'm not a Sunday school teacher you know. And I'm not going to turn into a junkie just by trying one of your Es. Did you?"

"What?"

"Turn into a junkie?"

"Of course not, I just don't want you to be…Sullied."

"Sullied!?" laughed Katie hysterically. "You didn't seem to have a problem with sullying me last night."

Tommy smirked. "Fair enough."

"If we take the odd one together, where's the harm? Just a social thing, like a glass of wine."

"Mmmm."

"Let's take them tomorrow night and we can watch the film."

Checkmate.

CHAPTER 42

Stevie had spent the previous few days holed up in his room. Boredom filled days waiting for a knock at the door or the interest to subside. The fact that there was a witness and Stevie had been spoken to by the police hours before troubled him. Would they make the connection? He also knew he had to get back out selling, or his customers would vanish. Eventually deciding to gamble on a heavy growth and a hoodie to keep him out of jail, he set out.

He hadn't gone far when he was confronted by a poster on the side of a bus shelter headed: "Wanted for Questioning," before detailing the crime. Most of the space however was taken up by an artist's impression which to his relief, even he didn't recognize. "Who's that ugly bugger? Eh, Stan?" Stevie felt himself relax and with a hi ho, it was off to work he went. As it turned out, it was pretty much business as usual. Any queries about where he had been were put down to illness, with an occasional discount for any particularly disgruntled regulars. As the mid-morning lull arrived, Stevie took a seat on the pavement next to Stan, picking him up and sitting him on his lap. As they sat there in ear tickling, tail wagging, face licking bliss, Stevie felt more content than he had for a long time. Maybe there was hope for some sort of future after all. But with his guard down and his hood up, he was caught unawares by the black BMW, which screeched to a halt in front of him. A curiously nimble man-mountain leapt out and grabbed Stevie by the arm and before he knew it they were side by side on the back seat, accelerating off to who knows where. In the front were another two men, late twenties, early thirties, smartly dressed.

"What's going on? I haven't done anything. I told you lot yesterday, I'm just selling the Big Issue," protested Stevie.

"What do you mean, you lot?" asked his neighbour.

"You…Cops…yesterday," he stammered. This seemed to amuse Stevie's hosts. But only briefly. These weren't cops. Stevie wished they were.

"You've been selling on our patch, interfering with our business," hissed the front seat passenger menacingly.

"I didn't know. I'll move somewhere else."

"There is no somewhere else, it's all mine, understand you little cunt?"

"Look…why don't…" Stevie searched desperately for a way out.

"Why don't you shut the fuck up?"

"We could do a deal; my stuffs just about ran out. I could sell for you."

"You mean like a merger?"

"Exactly! A merger," replied Stevie, hopefully.

"A merger, eh? I was thinking more of a takeover myself. A very hostile takeover."

The look in his eyes left Stevie in no doubt of his intensions.

"Say another word, you get stabbed."

Stevie watched out the window as the surroundings became less familiar and more remote. Regrets and "if only's" filled him as the life that had seemed so worthless just a short time ago suddenly became priceless, brimming with unfulfilled potential. Eventually they came to a halt next to a derelict building. Stevie looked around for signs of life, witnesses, but knew there were none. Would it be a violent warning? Or worse?

"Out!"

Stevie complied, opening the door. But as all four got out, Stevie decided to take the chance. Thankfully he hadn't been able to bring himself to part with his beloved knife, and he reached forward and slashed at the neck of his tormentor, before running as fast as he could for the trees. The sound of a crack and whistle past his ear eliminated any doubts he had made the right decision. He looked round as he ran, and saw to his relief that they had abandoned any thought of chase to tend to their stricken leader. Stevie kept running until he was far enough away as to be safely hidden but close enough to keep his captors under surveillance. It soon became obvious that gangster number 1 was in a bad way, and Stevie began to relax as he watched them load him hurriedly into the back of the car and speed off. He waited cautiously for a few minutes before breaking cover and heading back the way he came. It was going to be a long walk, and was going back to the hostel a smart idea? If they'd been watching him would they know where he lived? They could be waiting for him. But where else could he go?

Two hours later, he finally reached familiar territory. As he walked on, the smell of pizza from a take away up ahead was a sharp reminder that he hadn't eaten all day. His pace quickened. Reaching the shop, in its window he saw the same poster he'd seen earlier. Still unrecognisable he decided to go in but then, through the glass he suddenly found himself staring at a more familiar face. There, standing in the queue, paying for his pizza was James Paterson. Stevie didn't believe it at first, it couldn't be. But it was him, no doubt, looking more tanned, but it was him. Stevie stepped back away from the window, but knew he would be out any second. Quickly he sat down on the pavement, pulled his hood up and held out his hand. JP walked straight past. Stevie had learned that there is no one more invisible than a stranger asking for money. After he'd gone fifty yards up the road, Stevie got up and followed. He didn't have far to go. Two minutes later, James opened the door to a ground floor flat and was gone. Stevie slowly approached the door. Number 154.

"Later."

CHAPTER 43

As Stevie reached the top of the stairs, Stan, who'd been lying outside their door, ran towards him barking frantically. Stevie didn't care about the noise, he was just relieved. "You're like Grey Friars Bobby, eh wee man?" However, their happiness was temporarily interrupted by some barking from behind.

"No fucking animals in here, you know the rules."

Stevie turned and did what he wanted to do on day one. The punch broke the commandant's nose (Stevie never bothered to find out his name), and sent him head over heels down the stairs.

"Prick...Time for us to be moving on, Stan." Stevie had already decided it was too risky to hang around. Besides, there was no way he could deal anywhere nearby, so there was no reason to stay. Ten minutes later, Stevie had packed and they were gone. But to where? It was too late for trains and buses. There was also James Paterson to deal with. He'd still to figure out what to do there. After walking a bit further, he decided to spend a couple of days at a small hotel he knew on the outskirts of town. He'd try to chill out and think things through. So, on they walked, with Stevie on the lookout for a taxi, before convincing himself they were probably all owned by his captors to launder money. Finally, two sore feet and four sore paws later, they reached the Soprano Court Hotel. The name made Stevie nervous. "Bada fucking Bing," he muttered to himself. However, any worries that this was some gangster humour were eased by the silver haired old gent at the desk. He didn't look like the type to be packing heat under the counter.

"Could I have a room for a couple of nights?" The old man looked at Stan, then at Stevie.

"They don't allow pets here...but fuck 'em. He's a nice little dog eh? Two nights you say."

"Yeh," said Stevie, grinning.

"It's £30 a night."

"That's fine."

"Just fill in the form, son."

When he'd finished signing in, he pushed the form back across the desk.

"Room 36, upstairs. It's one of these stupid bloody plastic key things. Just stick it in, pull it out and try not to break it. Breakfast is seven till nine. Just keep Toto there off the bed, the maid will see the hairs and she's a right bitch."

"Cheers." As Stevie made his way to his room the old gent picked up the form.

"John Wayne, eh?" the man smiled. "That'll be the day."

Every floorboard and every step creaked as he made his way past the junk shop art, hanging skewed on artexed walls that hadn't seen fresh paint for decades. But at £30 a night Stevie didn't care. A bed and a locked door was all he was after. Counting down the room numbers as he went, he finally reached number 36. Slipping the plastic card into the slot and pulling it out, he ignored the little red light, turned the handle and pushed, but the door stood its ground. He tried again, withdrawing the card quicker this time. Again the door remained locked. He next left the card in the lock and pulled at the door. No joy. Finally, just before he was ready to kick the door in, he found a tight spot in the slot and pushed it that little bit further before pulling it out. A green light! He stood savouring the moment for a second, before turning the handle again and walking straight into the door almost breaking his nose. "Fuck!" he roared in pain and frustration. As he'd savoured, the lock had grown bored and turned red once more unnoticed, but he knew he had the beating of it. One more go and he was in, throwing his bag on the floor and Stan on the bed. "Fuck the maid," he muttered. Stevie paid no attention to his beige, basic surroundings as he turned, put the do not disturb sign on the handle outside, locked the door, put the chain on and joined Stan on the bed. Seconds later they were both asleep, snoring in perfect harmony, all night long.

"Bastard", muttered Stevie at the watch telling him breakfast had finished an hour ago. It was ten am and he was starving. He swung his legs over the side of the bed and sat up, rubbing his eyes, sighing as he got up and went into the bathroom, swaying groggily. Bladder emptied, he turned on the tap and washed his hands and face, the brain fog slowly dispersing.

251

Ten minutes later, he sat dressed, watching the news on the beat up portable TV in the corner trying to figure out what to do next. He suddenly found himself overwhelmed, as just how fucked up his life had become came into sharp focus. He'd managed to deal with little pocket-sized crises as they came along, pushing anything else to the back of his mind to be dealt with later. But now, all those little dramas had conspired to revolt, to break out into full, in your face consciousness. Deliberately or not, he'd killed people, he was on the run, could never go home. His family, friends, what had he done to them? Any future which could be considered normal in any way, shape or form was gone. He was always going to be alone and looking over his shoulder. But as panic gripped him he was pulled back from meltdown by more mundane matters. Stan needed a crap. "Ok buddy, let's take care of business," whispered Stevie softly to his whimpering companion. He gently picked him up and put him into his holdall, zipping it up, but leaving a few inches open. "Keep quiet, ok?" But he needn't have worried. The corridors and reception were deserted as he exited to a bright, crisp spring morning. Even the streets were deserted as he looked around for grassy knolls and hit men behind bushes. Seeing none, he lifted Stan out, who immediately dumped what seemed like half his body weight on the pavement. "Geez Stan, what the fuck you been eating?"

Stan stepped back to gaze at his handiwork with a mixture of pride and astonishment before having a sniff. Satisfied that it was dead, he walked on.

"Walkies, eh? Fair enough." Stevie began to relax as his paranoia dissipated. Up ahead he saw a shop, pacifying his now growling stomach. Ali's store was a glorified newsagent, which also met the basic grocery needs. Milk, bread of the cheap, processed to hell variety, cereal, about a hundred different kinds of sweets, smokes, and cheap booze guaranteed to give the maximum bang for your buck. It also boasted a top shelf that would make Charlie Sheen blush. Among the myriad of bizarre titles, one stood out. As he began flicking through "Dunkin dildos", his train of thought was interrupted by a high-pitched voice from behind.

"This isn't a library; we do sell them you know. I don't want sweat marks on it. Buy it or put it back."

"Calm down Ali, I though you Muslims were supposed to be against all this filth. Just trying to corrupt us infidels so you can get heaven to yourselves, eh?"

The shopkeeper smiled. "I don't think I'll be seeing you there."

"No, you'll be too busy getting a pitch fork up your arse down the other place!"

"Cheeky bastard!" laughed Ali.

"You got any sandwiches?"

"There's some in the fridge up the back. You going to buy them or just have a sneaky peak at those to?"

"Depends on what you got." A minute later, Stevie dropped a pack of cheese and tomato on the counter."

"Can you give me a half bottle of wine too?"

"What age are you?"

"Seventy-four."

"I see you've had a bit of work done."

"So, do you take a drink yourself?"

"No, no. No alcohol, no drugs, just a cup of tea."

"No drugs? And I had you down as a Rohypnol man. See you later." When Stevie got outside he opened the wine and kept walking. As he drank and walked and walked and drank, the wine began warming his belly. A few inches further south, the memories of dunking dildos was having a similar effect. It was no coincidence therefore that he found himself walking in the direction of the town's red light district. Ducking up an alley he paused to drain the last of the wine, tossed the empty bottle, unzipped his jeans and drained his bladder. He was now ready for action. Up ahead he saw a girl standing at the corner. Opposite was a short, stocky guy who had now locked onto him. As Stevie approached the girl, the man whistled and ushered him over. Stevie complied. As he got closer he realised that what he thought was short black hair was actually very elaborate tattoos all over his head and neck. Further study was cut short.

"What do you want?"

"Eh, are you with her?"

"No. She's with me. I'll ask you again. What do you want?"

"Eh, sex."

"Fuck sake. I didn't think you wanted flying lessons. What do you want to do to her?"

Stevie paused for a second to think. "How much for a blow job?"

"Twenty quid with a condom, forty without," came the reply, his voice now businesslike. As it had been a while, and the wine had brought Mr Fuck It out to play, Stevie decided to treat himself. As he handed over four ten pound notes, the man signalled to the girl, holding up four fingers.

"On you go now. She knows what to do. Enjoy."

As he approached her he almost changed his mind. Crowned by badly dyed blond hair, life had taken a heavy toll. She looked late twenties, but he'd seen what drink, drugs and sleeping rough could do to people, and even the oversized sunglasses couldn't hide the bruises beneath. His reservations were put to the side as she took his hand and led him round the corner into the alleyway. Reaching forward to touch her breast, he was soon reminded that this was not a date, or even a drunken fumble with a piece of Saturday night strange, the lucky man's kebab. No, before his hand got anywhere near its target, the girl was on her knees taking care of business, mechanical, cold, distant, like a wind-up sex toy. He'd bought her young, worn out body, but flesh wasn't enough. Stevie wanted more. Grabbing her hair, he tipped her head back. The girl gasped, confused and afraid.

"Look at me," he told her.

The girl acquiesced and began again. He looked down, peering through the tinted lenses, looking for a spark of humanity behind the vacant emotionless gaze, a connection. Balancing his attention between remaining aroused but resisting climax, he reached down and removed her glasses...and wished he hadn't. Stevie looked into her eyes, eyes as cold and dead as you'd find in any fishmongers window, and had his connection. He recoiled back, unable to breathe, shoving his withering lust back under cover, desperate to hide his shame. He paused, till his trembling voice asked what he already knew.

"Susie? ...Is that you?"

The girl, looked up, a dim ray of awareness trying to break through the fog.

"Was I not doing it right?.... do I know you?"

"No! No you don't!"

Stevie turned and ran, but as he neared the end of the alley the tattooed man blocked his path.

"What the fuck did you do!?"

Stevie took all the money he had in his pocket, thrust it into the man's hand and ran. He kept on running as the man counted out about £200, shaking his head, smiling.

"Some crazy fuckers in this world," he said as he watched Stevie disappear. "Hope he didn't kill her."

CHAPTER 44

Fuelled by desperation, Stevie ran and ran, frantically trying to put as much distance as he could between him and those eyes. Those eyes that once sparkled with such innocent fun, that looked up to him, not as they had moments before, but as a child taking her first tentative, flirtatious steps into the grown up world, un scarred and carefree. But no speed could outrun her, or the truth now breaking free from the recess in which he'd tried to bury it, but which was now burying him. His self-pity was swept aside by guilt for the lives he'd ruined. Their broken dreams and stolen futures demanded to be acknowledged, growing impossible to ignore with every desolate step. Tommy's mum and dad, Tommy, Susie, even James Paterson. All victims. His victims.

As he gave up hope of escape, Stevie suddenly found himself facing the hotel entrance. The end of the line. Not knowing what else to do, where else to go, he headed back to his room. Stan, out of breath, followed unnoticed. He closed the door behind him and stood perfectly still. Darkness had emptied him. He sat on the bed, head in hands and wept. Stan jumped up, licking the tears as they fell. "You're a good boy Stan, but I'm done."

In the silence he sat, his mind shut down, one hour, two hours, anguish tightening its noose. Eventually he summoned the energy to stand

and switch on the TV, a distraction to relieve the pain, but there was no respite. His life was destroyed beyond repair and his inevitable mistakes to come were just going to prolong the pain and suffering of those he cared about. He took out the knife from his pocket, playing with it slowly, feeling the razor sharp edge that had severed life from its earthly garb just days earlier. As he sat resigned, his attention was distracted by the afternoon matinee movie beginning. "The Searchers", Tommy and his favourite film, watching it so many times they could recite most of the dialogue, and frequently did. Neither he nor Tommy knew why, it just seemed to touch something in them, a common place in two very disparate souls. The film starred John Wayne as Ethan Edwards, a confederate soldier searching for his niece taken by an Apache raiding party and wrestling with his own demons along the way, the outcome always uncertain. As the film began, his heart ached for a glimpse of redemption. As the closing credits rolled, he knew what he had to do.

CHAPTER 45

James Paterson froze as he opened the door. Adrenaline dumped into his bloodstream, but he knew neither fight nor flight would change a damn thing. It was over.

"What do you wa-"

Before he could complete his pointless question, Stevie had stepped past him.

"Don't mind if I do." Finding the living room, he sat on the arm of the black leather armchair and looked at the carpet. Stan sat on the floor by his side. James stood for a moment before dropping onto the settee, swinging his legs up, and leaning back.

"All the gin joints in all the world, eh? How did you find me?"

Stevie remained silent, still staring at the floor.

"I only got back a few days ago, Thursday. You been watching the airports? Did you know I was in Ireland? What? Couldn't afford the fare to go over and hunt me down there?" Silence. "Ok no more chewing the fat, let's get to it. How much do you want? I assume in the absence of the police, you've come for the money? Well don't believe what you read in the papers, there wasn't that much. Yeah, a few grand, but mainly I just wanted to get the fuck away from the wife, clean start. You've no fucking idea. A total gold digger. All my mates warned me but, hey, the power of the furry magnet eh…well, until she shaved it, but she was something else in that department, until we got married but….anyway, what I'm saying is, I'm no fucking millionaire so-"

"Those were nice dogs in that photo on your desk," interrupted Stevie.

"What?"

"In the photo on your desk, that day I visited. Your family and some dogs."

"Yeah. The dogs," mumbled James baffled. "You know, they're the only thing I miss. Not the wife, not the kids, just the dogs. How fucked up is that?"

"What kind were they?"

"Just mongrels. The wife hated that, stuck up bitch. She wanted poodles. That was one time I stood up to her. Instant celibacy for that though. But was she going to take them for walks? Can you imagine the crap you'd get? A man walking poodles. "

"Yeah, you might as well cut the arse out your pink satin hot pants and let them get on with it, eh." Replied Stevie quietly, mind elsewhere.

"Exactly. No, give me my pick and mix mutts any day. Miss them so I do…Anyway you're not here to talk about dogs, you're here to talk about money."

"Actually, I'm here to talk about dogs. Or rather a dog." He picked up Stan and sat him on his knee. As he stroked his ears, Stan jumped up to lick Stevie's face. "The best dog in the whole wide world, aincha Stan my man?"

"I don't understand."

"Do you want to go to jail James?"

"Well no, obviously."

"Don't get lippy James. You don't want to go to jail...obviously, but I could send you there, or to hell in a helicopter for that matter."

James looked even more confused.

"No, I don't know where that came from either, but that's neither here nor there. The point is this. You can stay out of jail, and keep your money. Well most of it. It's not what I want."

"What do you want?"

"I want you to look after this little chap."

Now it was James turn to fall silent.

"Do we have a deal, James?"

"I still don't understand."

"There's nothing to understand, James. You like dogs, yes?"

"Yes"

"You want to stay out of jail?"

"Yes"

"You want to keep most of your money?"

"...Yes"

"Well sounds like a fucking home run to me, poodle boy."

"But why?"

"I don't have time for why's, or any other fucking questions except do we have a deal?"

"Eh, yeah, sure."

"Now here are the rules. Very simple rules. First, if you dump him, harm him or take inadequate care of him, you shall go to jail or be killed, depending on who gets to you first. Second. He doesn't eat any old thing. Only the best. He gets the same meat you eat. Steak, chicken, breast only, no bones in case he chokes, some fish. In an absolute emergency an occasional bowl of Whiskas may be acceptable, but if he runs away trouble's coming James. Lastly, I hear all your crap about only getting away with twenty pounds and a postal order, but we know that isn't true, don't we James? I know when little Stan here's let one go and I know the smell of bullshit, and right now Stan's smelling prettier than a thousand dollar whore."

Stan's tail wagged at the compliment.

"That's from 'Blaz-"

"Yes I know it's from 'Blazing Saddles', but anyway-"

"But-"

"No butts James, not even in pink hot pants. Now I reckon you got away with at least half a million."

James again tried to interrupt.

"Are we butting James? I thought we were clear on that. But I don't want half a million, James. One hundred grand. A mere twenty percent finder's fee. Now does this all seem reasonable, James? A good deal? Freedom, wealth and man's best friend. Not a bad evening's work."

"It'll take a few days to get the money," said James, still suspicious.

"Not a problem. I don't want it anyway. Have it delivered to this address in two weeks' time. If you don't..."

"Yeah, yeah, I go to jail."

Stevie pulled out his knife. "Not necessarily."

James paled at the sight of the glistening blade. "I'll do what you say."

262

"Make sure you do." Stevie picked up the dog and handed him over. As James held him, he too received the Stan face wash.

"He's cute," laughed James.

"Yes.... Yes he is. Remember, no crap. Bye Stan," he whispered.

"I'll see myself out." As he did, he stopped at the living room door and turned. You were right, James. It was my fault."

CHAPTER 46

As the sun began to fade the sky changed colour, its red light tinting the earthly world below, hinting at the myriad of pleasures playing out behind the shades, and in the shadows and minds beneath. The air was crisp, silent and tense as high-noon. Stevie walked slowly, purposefully into the only part of this red light world he was interested in. The street was deserted, business slow. But tonight he was only playing the part of a punter. Entering stage left with stealth and guile, he caught the pimp by surprise.

"What the fuck do you want?" he asked, startled embarrassment turning to anger.

"Now I ask you, is that any way to talk to the paying public on a quiet night such as this?"

"I'll ask you one last time asshole, what do you want?"

Stevie put his right hand into his pocket, eyes fixed on the pimp's, a slight smile turning the corners of his mouth. The pimp tensed, trying to read the situation, not sure what was going on. He thought about lashing out, but fear and greed staid his hand. Stevie felt the knife, the comfort and security of an old comrade. 'Stand, down soldier'.

"I want to fuck yer bitch up Mr Pimp dude, but it's a little bit chilly out, so..."

"Who the fuck you calling a pimp!?"

"I'm sorry. Does this fall under the social services mandate now? Meals on wheels a bit passé?"

"Listen cunt, I'm warning you!"

Just at that, Stevie pulled out a fist full of dollars, or £500 to be more accurate, accrued from his days as drug baron.

"Half a grand to fuck her in the comfort of my own centrally heated, tastefully furnished, love shack baby. I'll bring her back in the morning, rested, washed and ready for another day at the office. I'll even throw in a bowl of cornflakes. Now, how does that sound?"

The pimp relaxed at the sight of the money, now in more familiar territory.

"And why don't I just take the money, asshole?" he sneered.

Stevie returned his hand to his pocket and the smile to his face. "Because that would be bad for business."

As they locked glares, eye wrestling for a moment, the pimp sensed real danger. He let out a face saving chuckle. "Woo, I'm scared to death."

"It tends to be bit messier than that...but I digress, do we have a deal?"

The pimp sensed he didn't have a choice. Stevie knew he didn't.

"Ok, ok, what the fuck, just have her back by morning."

"Yeah, yeah, like I said, washed, waxed and a full tank of gas."

"Eh?"

"Nothing, just get her over here."

The pimp took the money and waved her over. The girl that was Susie didn't budge, even though she appeared to be looking right at them.

"Hey, Candy, get fucking over here you stupid bitch."

Stevie's hand tightened on the knife still hidden in his pocket, desperate to lunge forward, but he maintained control, took his hand off the knife and relaxed. The girl registered the noise and ambled towards them. As she reached them she struggled to focus on the night's trick, before returning to detached indifference.

"This guy's gonna take real good care of you ok, so you go with him, ok, baby doll?"

The girl shrugged, looking into the distance. Stevie put his arm round her waist, gently drawing her close, and holding her steady. "Yeah, don't worry; I'll take care of you now," whispered Stevie softly in her ear.

They walked off the way he had come, deliberately, in no hurry. He knew he still had matters to attend to, but as he held the prize in his arms, he was content to savour the moment. Red sky at night had brought this shepherd delight. As he reached the end of the street he turned back to face the pimp.

"Say goodbye, honey."

"Goodbye honey," she answered obediently.

Stevie sighed and pulled her closer. "Soon you'll be free from all the shit of this world." He led her across the road, deserted except for the red Ford focus he had "borrowed" earlier. He opened the passenger door and helped her in. As he leaned across to fasten her seatbelt, he turned to face her, stroking her cheek. He sang softly. "Thought of you as my mountaintop, thought of you as my peak, though of you as just about everything I had, but couldn't keep, I had but couldn't keep. Linger on, your pale blue eyes." As he sang the Velvet Underground classic, Susie seemed to smile, to recognize the song she'd heard so many times through Stevie's bedroom door. "Linger on darling," he whispered, kissing her on the forehead. He closed the door, walked round the car, and then stopped to stare up at the night sky, smiling, grateful. He then got in, and they drove off.

Mile after mile they drove in holy, reverent silence, through hushed amber-lit streets as the residents, hidden co-conspirators, left the players to the final inevitable act. Dusk faded and street lights were left behind as they drove steady and straight into the darkness, beyond the desperate soap opera lives and prying eyes, speeding up as the road narrowed into winding country lanes, faster and faster, cutting across bends, wheel clenched tight, teeth clenched tighter. As they flew, Stevie turned towards his passenger for a second, her gaze unconcerned, long past caring what lay around any corner, swaying limply through the bends. As he returned his eyes to the road he jerked the wheel just in time, a hairpin bend suddenly upon them. "Keep your eyes on the road, your hands upon the wheel," he sang softly, breaking the silence.

On and on he drove, gear crunching rally-style as the road wound through the shrouded woodlands. Suddenly he jammed his foot down hard on the brakes, skidding into a clearance beneath the green leaf canopy. He turned off the engine and got out quickly, staring deep into the dense forest. Outside, leaves whispered in the wind, insects scratched and buzzed, birds settled down for the night. Inside...inside, there was mental static, feint, all thoughts subdued, redundant. His thinking had been done. He breathed in deeply, the air pure, cleansing, as he looked up once more into the sparkling void, minute after minute, rapt, clear. Sighing, he got back into the car.

"What do you want me to do?" whispered his passenger.

"Not a thing Susie Q, not a thing."

He opened the window. Outside, the autumn leaves, stiff and decayed, rustled their farewells before their inevitable fall to the mass grave below. Oblivious, Stevie reached into his pocket. Susie's eye's followed; showing no fear as the knife appeared, resting in his upturned palm. He caressed it with his thumb and turned to her. "Time to cut the past adrift."

CHAPTER 47

"Stevie! Where have you..." Tommy stopped abruptly, words put aside as he became aware of the ghost behind his prodigal friend. For a moment time stopped.

"Susie? Stevie....is it? " He asked, his voice barely audible, pleading. "Oh my God," his voice louder. He stepped closer, stopping as she appeared to flinch, watching her anxiously as she stared past him into the house behind him, as if regaining consciousness. He moved forward again, slowly this time, taking her hand gently as she looked tentatively towards his eyes.

"Tommy?" she whispered.

He pulled her tight against him, daring the world to snatch her back. Tears burst free, washing away the anguish he feared he'd carry to his grave. "What's happened to her, where has she been, how-?"

"Don't ever ask me...long as you live; don't ever ask me more." interrupted Stevie.

Tommy looked him in the eye, recognising the familiar line, puzzled, but too overwhelmed by events to enquire further. Hand round her waist, he led her inside, gently supporting her every, weary step. He turned his head to speak to his friend, but he wasn't there. He stopped and looked back to see Ethan Edwards silhouetted in the doorway, left arm across his body holding the right hanging by his side. The Stetson was missing, but Tommy immediately recognised John Wayne's iconic closing shot.

"Take care of her...of each other."

"Aren't you coming in?" asked Tommy, knowing the answer.

Stevie shook his head. "One more thing to take care of. Tell mum I love her."

Reaching in, he pulled the door closed, watching as they vanished.

CHAPTER 48

Stevie opened the door of the police station and moved steadily towards the reception counter. A tall female officer glanced up as he approached.

"Can I help you?" she asked with practised interest.

"I want to talk to someone about a hit and run, and...well let's start with that."

The policewoman, now with genuine interest, looked him up and down for a hint of recognition, trying to decide if he was for real. Something in Stevie's demeanour told her he was.

"Take a seat sir; someone will attend to you in a moment."

He turned and sat, sinking deep into the upholstered chair, yet feeling lighter, less burdened than he had for a long, long time. He pulled out a cigarette and lit up.

"Eh, excuse me, but you can't smoke in here!" spluttered the dumb founded policewoman.

Stevie smiled. "How about we just add it to the list."

###

Thank you for reading my book. If you enjoyed it, won't you please take a moment to leave me a review at the retailers? We independent writers need all the support we can get.

Thanks!

Robert Cowan

Acknowledgements

The Family
My wife, Carol , son Keith, daughter Fern and my astonishing good luck for having you.
Jan and Boaby, for always being there when needed.
Mum and Dad (Who would be appalled by the language and subject matter)
Dr James and team Columbus (who hopefully won't be).

The Crew
For an almost 40 year adventure
Boab Douglas (thanks for the cover art)
John Cunningham
Billy Forsyth
Jim Duffy
Ricky Forsyth
Wilson Galloway
James "JimBob" Galloway
The Rolling Stones (they need the publicity)

Despatches
For pain and gain:
Lanarkshire Kapap
Kapap UK

Beyond
The Bhudda
The Dhamma
The Sangha
And all who seek their better nature (Ethan?)

About The Author

Well...what about me? I was born in Bellshill which seems to have been a hotbed of creativity. Not sure why, maybe we feel we have something to prove. Nowadays I live in Lesmahagow with my wife and two children, working as a design engineer. For fun I drum, strum and write stuff like this. Also a fan of martial arts, but got old! (See acknowledgements / despatches for recommendations if you're into such things)

I'm currently working on two more books which I hope to finish before I die. With your support I'm sure I'll get there. Check on my Amazon page for updates.

PS. I don't have a terminal illness, but what's a novel without melodrama. Anyway, enough!

CPSIA information can be obtained at www.ICGtesting.com
Printed in the USA
LVOW10s2201120715

445980LV00004B/141/P